"Can't stay here . . ." he thought when a part of him wanted to give up and go to sleep. "Can't stay. Gotta . . . gotta move . . . until I can't move . . . no more . . ."

Longarm got up and began running blindly along the side of the tracks. He had no idea which direction to head, so he decided to head in the same direction as the train. Eventually, he would reach a settlement. Maybe not for many yards, possibly not for many miles. But it was as good a direction as any.

And he had nothing else to do—except lie down and die.

He ran for maybe twenty yards. And then his numb feet stopped working, as did his numb legs, his numb knees. His numb brain. He fell and then he rolled down the slope to pile up in a large, downy pillow of snow to sleep that last, long cold sleep in the chilly palm of the cosmos' massive hand . . .

TABOR EVANS

LONGARM

AND THE COLDEST TOWN IN HELL

JOVE BOOKS, NEW YORK

THE BERKLEY PUBLISHING GROUP
Published by the Penguin Group
Penguin Group (USA) LLC
375 Hudson Street, New York, New York 10014

USA • Canada • UK • Ireland • Australia • New Zealand • India • South Africa • China

penguin.com

A Penguin Random House Company

LONGARM AND THE COLDEST TOWN IN HELL

A Jove Book / published by arrangement with the author

For information, address: The Berkley Publishing Group,
a division of Penguin Group (USA) LLC,
375 Hudson Street, New York, New York 10014.

ISBN: 978-0-515-15435-1

PUBLISHING HISTORY
Jove mass-market edition / June 2014

PRINTED IN THE UNITED STATES OF AMERICA

10 9 8 7 6 5 4 3 2 1

Cover illustration by Milo Sinovcic.

Chapter 1

Three days before Christmas, Jenny Tallant, owner of the Blue Dog Saloon in Little Missouri City, which lay like a snow-buried trash heap in the bluffs of western Dakota Territory, had been nervous all day long. Why that was so, she wasn't certain.

It could have been that she was sixty-two years old and her bursitis was acting up again in her left shoulder. Or that she was sixty-two years old and she'd been living alone too long in her two-room shack behind the saloon, which was on the other side of the river and obscured by a fringe of ancient cottonwoods.

Jenny's life mate, Abigail Landry, with whom she had run the Blue Dog for over twenty years, had been swaddled in a six-foot-deep hole on the side of Indian Butte for the past five years. When you were sixty-two and you'd been living alone for five years in a town of two hundred, in a town that was frozen up solid and buried under three feet of snow for five months every year—a town that was a good two days' ride from any-place of any significance whatever—you were bound to get spooked now and then.

Downright nervous for no apparent reason.

Cabin fever was likely all it was, Jenny silently opined as she ran a damp cloth across her oak bar, though she'd performed the same maneuver three times in the past hour despite the fact that the bar was as clean as a parson's prayer. Jenny looked at the old Regulator clock hanging above the back bar mirror over her left shoulder.

Two thirty-three.

She hadn't had a customer since twelve thirty, and then it had only been the town constable, Emmitt Grassley, who'd come in for his noon beer and to build a ham sandwich from the free lunch platter Jenny usually kept to lure in customers, few as there were in these parts in the middle of another gall dang, cold-assed Dakota winter. Fairly frequently, the town's most recent widower, Franklin Talbot, who ran Talbot's Tack and Feed, came in to pony up a dollar to spend with Jenny's only doxy, Miss Evangeline Van Dyke.

That was the doxy's real name, and she'd even grown up in these parts and been a schoolteacher before the school closed from lack of interest. Her family was dead—they'd dropped one by one over the years, like flies at the first frost. As practical as she was pretty, rather than leave Little Missouri City to brave what could possibly have been a harsher life somewhere out in the vast unknown, Miss Evangeline came to work for Jenny for an 80/20 percent split of her profits and for free room and board in one of Jenny's stark upstairs rooms.

It beat a life in Minot or Bismarck, Jenny figured, where the pretty young woman would likely be spreading her legs for less money and a lower breed of john who'd probably give her the clap or something even more wretched. She was likely better off here in most ways, but Jenny wasn't sure how Miss Evangeline stood the boredom.

At the moment the ex-schoolteacher was laying out a game of solitaire at a table near the fully stoked woodstove and a piñon pine sporting five silver strands of Christmas tinsel. Miss Evangeline was attired in a metallic green dress with a shawl that Jenny had knit for her draped about her otherwise bare shoulders. Her thick brown hair was pulled back behind her pretty, finely featured face and wound into a near-perfect French braid. She'd painted her lips a lush crimson, though she otherwise needed little face paint.

Beautiful woman, Jenny thought, tapping her thick, callused fingers on the bar. Oh, to be twenty, thirty years younger . . .

Jenny sighed and glanced at the clock again. Two minutes later than the last time she'd looked. You knew it was a slow day when Miss Evangeline couldn't even pull in Franklin Talbot or one of the least bashful of her ex-students who enjoyed the novelty of fucking their teacher.

Jenny heard the muffled drum of hooves in the snow.

Miss Evangeline looked up from her card game, frowned speculatively at Jenny, and then both women turned their gazes to the brightly lit front windows on either side of the saloon's closed winter doors. The light off the snow was so brilliant that Jenny not only had to squint but shade her eyes with her hand. As she did, the drumming grew louder until three riders swaddled in heavy furs, their breath steaming whitely in the dazzling sunshine, appeared on the street, heading from left to right, south to north. They didn't continue heading north, however, but swerved their horses up to the hitchrack fronting the Blue Dog.

"Well, I'll be," Jenny said, her heart lightening. "We might just turn a couple of dimes or even quarters yet today, Miss Evangeline!"

But then that pain in Jenny's shoulder reared its ugly head again. She winced. Her strange sense of unease returned, and she thought it was no coincidence that it had intensified the moment she saw the three riders, their faces concealed by heavy black, red, or blue scarves wrapped around their heads against the near-zero cold, pull their horses up to her hitchrack.

They were all big men, she saw as they swung down from their saddles. Big men in rough, heavy winter clothing. Ominous bulges in their coats showed where they were carrying guns. At nearly the same time, all three shucked rifles from their saddle scabbards and rested said rifles on their shoulders as they climbed the porch's three steps single file, boots thumping on the cold, half-rotten boards that complained loudly against the sudden weight.

Jenny shared another glance with Miss Evangeline. The former schoolteacher's expression was hopeful, but then, apparently seeing the unease in Jenny's eyes, Miss Evangeline frowned. Jenny wanted to hurry the young woman upstairs, to get her out of possible harm's way. But then the cowbell over the door jangled and the door scraped and rattled open, letting in a blast of cold air as the three rough riders stomped into the room. They all smelled of the sour scents of unbathed men and horses and fetid hides and furs and cold leather and steel.

The first man in the three-man group was shorter than the other two. As he walked to the bar, holding his rifle in one hand and unwrapping the scarf from around his face with the other hand, Jenny's guts clenched. The face suddenly exposed to her was the face of a wild animal more than that of a man. A degenerate. Vermin. She'd lived out here long enough to have known her share of gut wagon–prowling human dogs, but this man was the leader of the pack.

It wasn't so much the flatness and evilness fairly radiating from his yellow eyes; it was the aura he emanated. Like a stench even stronger than his sweat and wet hide smell. That aura caused the hair on the back of Jenny's neck to stick straight up in the air and for gooseflesh to rise between her shoulder blades.

She suppressed a shudder as the man set his rifle loudly down atop the bar, tossed his muffler onto the rifle, and said, looking right at Jenny, "My, my—that's a big, ugly woman."

The man directly behind him laughed. The other one snorted as he, too, set his rifle onto the bar and said, "Set us up, princess. Bottle of your best stuff. And how 'bout a deck of playin' cards?"

"You got it," Jenny said, not reacting to the slight. She wasn't accustomed to such direct insults, but she'd read the insults in many a man's eyes too many times over the years not to have acquired a thick skin concerning her looks.

The first man, the truly evil-looking one with his yellow eyes and frost-rimed, light red mustache that drooped down over the corners of his knife-slash mouth, turned toward Miss Evangeline. He pointed to the young woman, who was tensely staring down at her cards, and said, "Hey, that's the teacher who took up whorin', ain't it? We done heard about her all the way over Wyomin' way—purty-assed schoolteacher who started spreadin' her purty legs when her school closed down."

"That her?" said the man to his right, staring at Miss Evangeline. He'd just set his rabbit fur hat with earflaps onto the bar, and his black hair was matted to his long, narrow head except for a rooster tail at the crown. "That the one over there?"

Miss Evangeline raised a brow and spread her crimson lips with a friendly but guarded smile. "Hello, fellas. Yes, I'm the one, all right." She set a card down atop another one, and as she did so, she said, "You fellas heeled enough for a poke?"

That made Jenny's stomach tighten even more. She had a bad sense about all three of these men, and she didn't think it would be a good idea for Miss Evangeline to take one of them upstairs.

"How 'bout it, Drake?" the man with the black rooster tail asked the yellow-eyed evil one. "We got time?"

"Sure, we got time," Drake said, glancing back behind the bar at the Regulator clock. "The rest of the boys won't be here for a coupla hours. With all this snow, it might take 'em even longer—coupla days, maybe." He threw back the entire shot that Jenny had just poured for him, then slammed the glass back down on the counter. "But I do believe I'll be first. Don't like goin' after you, Vincent. Hell, you're liable to get so excited you'll cut the purty teacher's throat. What would that leave me?"

As he lifted his Stetson, the short, stocky Drake, with thighs the size of tree trunks, strode in his heavy, stomping way between the tables toward Miss Evangeline and ran a hand through his oily, sandy-colored hair. He set his hat back down on his head and then he reached down, lightning quick, and grabbed Miss Evangeline's right arm, jerking her rudely to her feet.

"Hey, stranger," intoned the former teacher, scowling at the man, her pretty cheeks flushed red with fear and anger. "Turn your horns in right now, or I'll be rescinding my invitation!"

Drake drew her toward him, laughing, and said, "You'll do *what* to your invitation?" He laughed and slid a slit-eyed, lewdly bright glance toward his pards at the bar. "Oh, I can see I'm gonna have me a grand old time fuckin' the teacher! Come on, teacher, get on upstairs and get out o' them duds. Why, I'm so horny I'm liable to rip 'em off and take you right here! Nothin' makes me hornier than a big-talkin' whore!"

Fury overwhelming Jenny, she slammed a bottle down hard on the bar and shouted, "That's *enough!* I will not have Miss Evangeline treated that way! Out! Out—all of you!"

Drake kept an iron grip on Miss Evangeline as he whipped around, a pistol instantly in his hand.

Bam!

The bullet shattered a shot glass sitting atop the pyramid to Jenny's right, within a foot of her right arm. Now,

Jenny had had lead directed her way before. But not that close. At least, not that close on purpose. She could tell that Drake—and just then she recognized him from the wanted dodgers that had been hanging over in the post office for the past year as the outlaw Emory Drake—had put that bullet right where he'd wanted to.

And she could tell by the flat, mean light in those hard yellow eyes as well as by the direction he was aiming his smoking six-shooter, sort of half-out from his belly, that he'd place the next one in Jenny's tired old ticker. Fear gripped her. She was accustomed to the sensation, which made it all the more powerful. She gasped and, hating herself for the way her knees had suddenly turned to mud, she raised her hands up by her shoulders, silently beseeching the notorious killer from over Wyoming way not to kill her.

At the same time, Miss Evangeline's own eyes were beseeching Jenny for help, which made Jenny feel all the more fearful, wretched, and helpless.

"Anything else out of that fat old cow," Drake snarled at the other two men, who were standing and grinning in delight at the recent events, "shoot her through that big ugly face of hers. Understand?"

"You got it, Drake," said the one who had not yet spoken. He was a redhead with a mess of freckles across his face and one wandering eye. That would be Curly Jenkins. Jenny recognized him now, too. His poster was also hanging in the post office, between Emory Drake's and the third man's, the one with the long, narrow head and the rooster tail, whose name eluded Jenny though Drake had addressed him as "Vincent."

Vincent McKirk? That would make sense. The three

had been known to ride together. They were mentioned in all the newspapers, which Jenny read when she could get them.

Drake holstered his pistol and gave Miss Evangeline a hard shove toward the stairs at the back of the room. Miss Evangeline screamed as she fell over a chair, and then she gave another, hoarse cry as Drake jerked her back to her feet, laughing, and slapped her hard across her cheek with the back of his hand.

"Please!" Jenny cried, unable to help herself. "Don't . . . don't hurt her. You don't have—!"

She stopped when she saw Curly Jenkins aiming a pistol at her, his own malicious eyes sparking nastily over the black steel barrel. Jenny wished she still had her old shotgun stowed away beneath the bar, but someone had swiped the big popper last summer and she hadn't yet replaced it. She doubted it would have helped her much against these three, but she still wished she had it.

Drake pushed Miss Evangeline up the stairs and out of sight, though Jenny could hear them thumping around up there, Miss Evangeline by turns pleading and screaming as they headed for her room. Jenny stood frozen. Finally, Jenkins holstered his pistol. He gave Jenny a devilish wink and then grabbed the bottle and deck of cards off the bar, and he and Vincent McKirk slacked into chairs around a table in the middle of the room, not far from the stairs.

Jenkins shuffled the deck. Meanwhile, Jenny continued to stand frozen in place, listening to the skirmishing on the second story, which died for a time.

And then the hard thumps of a headboard reached Jenny's ears—the metronomic hammerings of a man in the throes of violent passion. Miss Evangeline was sobbing. The sobs became anguished groans when Drake was especially violent. She screamed when the outlaw slapped her, and Jenny closed her eyes against the demon's ribald laughter.

She closed her eyes, felt the wetness of tears ooze out from beneath her eyelids to dribble down her cheeks.

Helpless.

She'd never felt so helpless.

Chapter 2

About a half hour after he'd gone up with Miss Evangeline, Drake came back downstairs with a big, wolfish grin on his face. "Next!" he said as he dropped down onto the saloon floor, buckling his cartridge belt and two six-shooters around his hard, thick waist.

"Christ," McKirk said, throwing his cards onto the table and rising. "Anything left of her?"

Jenny stood where she'd been standing before, digging her fingers into the edge of the bar top, her blood rushing through her veins. The din, including Miss Evangeline's sobs, had stopped only a moment ago, when Jenny had also heard the screeching of the springs that meant Drake was finally climbing off the poor girl.

"Ah, she's all right," Drake said, chuckling through his teeth and sliding Jenny a mocking grin. "Prob'ly won't be after you get done with her, Vincent."

"Hey, Vincent—let *me* go next!" urged the redhead, Curly Jenkins, rising from his chair.

Vincent was trudging a little drunkenly toward the stairs, snickering as he threw his long head back and said, "You can go fuck yourself, old pard. Me? Why, it's my turn to fuck the teach!"

Drake poured out a drink at the table where Jenkins had just slouched back down into his chair, and turned to Jenny. "Best be lookin' for a new girl, lady. You is a lady, ain't ya? Hard to tell from them overalls you're wearin'. Anyways, best be lookin' for a new girl, Whatever-You-Are. The one upstairs is about to get all used up. Vincent's got quite a way with women!"

Jenkins cursed.

Jenny lurched back in anger and then turned to start walking out from behind the bar.

"Uh-uh!" Drake said, clicking the hammer of his six-shooter back, which he'd unholstered and leveled at Jenny in a mind-numbing blur of quick motion. "I wouldn't do that, ugly woman. You just stay right where you are, less'n you want me to drill you a third eye!"

Jenkins looked up at Jenny, narrowing his seedy brown eyes and snickering, showing his two front teeth, one of which was only half there, leaving a jagged edge.

"You just stay there and set up another bottle. I'll come over and fetch it, save you a trip. You're so damn ugly, I don't want you to get that close."

Again, Jenkins snickered.

Jenny ground her back teeth against the insults and pulled another bottle off a back bar shelf. Meanwhile, the off-key singing of bedsprings and the miserable moaning began to emanate again through the ceiling over Jenny's head. She ground her molars harder and resisted the urge to spit in the face of Drake, who retrieved the fresh bottle from the bar. Drake rolled his eyes toward the ceiling, "Vincent's havin' him a fine old time up there, sure 'nough!"

"I hope not too fine!" said Jenkins, shuffling the card deck.

Jenny waited on pins and needles while McKirk finished up with Miss Evangeline. Then he came down, grinning lewdly and chuckling, and hooked his thumb over his shoulder for Jenkins to take his turn, which he did, to the same nerve-rending chorus in the ceiling. Jenkins wasn't up there for over fifteen minutes before he came back down, tying his green neckerchief around his neck.

As he headed for the table where the other two were playing cards, he looked at Jenny. "Don't worry. She's still got some skin on them fine bones of hers." He chuckled and then slacked down into a chair.

Jenny was about to hurry upstairs to see about Miss Evangeline, but then four more riders, coming into town from the north, swerved over to the hitchrack fronting the Blue Dog.

"That the boys?" asked Emory Drake, twisting around in his chair to look out the two front windows. The others looked, too, and then he turned to face the table again and said, "Nope. Ranch hands, looks like."

The three outlaws had resumed their card game when the four newcomers filed into the Blue Dog. They were dressed much like the three outlaws but a little less shabbily. Jenny's heart raced, skipping every other beat, when she recognized the first two men. Deputy U.S. marshals they were, Brian Blake and Hoot Williams out of the main territorial office in Bismarck. The fourth who came in was the foreman of the Double Bar T Ranch out west of Little Missouri City. Jenny did not recognize the third man until he'd taken off his woolen, frost-rimed, winter facemask. Then her heart fluttered and quickened even more when she recognized the county sheriff, handsome, gray-haired Lew Patten.

The federals and the local sheriff! Her wordless prayer had been answered!

"Well, well, well," Jenny intoned, trying her best to not start screaming and pointing out the three wanted outlaws who'd so poorly treated Miss Evangeline, "look what the cat dragged in." She glanced quickly at the outlaws, relieved to find them still very much involved in their card game, and then looked back at the lawmen. "What brings you boys out in all this snow and cold, way off here at the edge of the known world?"

Instantly, Jenny realized her mistake. If they told her what they were up to out here, which was most likely law business, they'd probably get bushwhacked by the three uncouth desperadoes sitting at their table near the stairs. Before the outlaws could learn that these men were lawmen, Jenny had to first warn them in some fashion, to in some subtle way draw their attention to the killers.

So, before any of the three could respond, she said, "Can I set you up with some firewater? You know I got the best tangleleg in three counties!" She laughed her usual, mannish laugh, though it sounded tinny to her own ears.

"Well, I wouldn't know about that, Miss Jenny," said

Sheriff Patten with a smile, tossing his hat and
wool mask onto the bar, "but you can set us up with
what you got, just the same. Gall dang, but it's cold out
there!"

"Too damn cold for these old bones, I'll tell you that,"
said Deputy U.S. Marshal Brian Blake, whom Jenny
guessed was in his fifties, though he wore his years deep
in the creases of his almost revoltingly weathered face.
"And if it wasn't for a handful of rustlers long-looping
Double Bar T cattle, we'd be home, sitting by a hot fire
and waiting out the winter."

Jenny laughed a little too woodenly at that. She
glanced over at the outlaws. Just then Drake turned to
look at her critically, and then he glanced over the four
newcomers, wrinkling the skin above the bridge of his
broad, pugnacious nose.

Jenny thought her heart stopped. Fashioning a stony
smile, she grabbed a bottle from under the bar and
popped the cork, wondering if she should just go ahead
and scream a warning to the lawmen now, and let the
chips fall where they may, or hope that Drake didn't get
savvy as to who the four newcomers were.

Sheriff Patten must have sensed Jenny's unease. The
sheriff suddenly turned to look at Jenny's three other
customers. Fortunately, just as he did so, Jenkins told
Drake it was Drake's call, and the thick man with the
evil yellow eyes turned back to the table, giving his
broad back to the bar, and resumed the poker game.
Jenny felt a slight ease in her tension, suspecting that if
either man had recognized the other one, all hell might
have broken loose right then and there.

She needed to convey to the lawmen the trouble here,

but she needed to do so in such a way that the outlaws didn't know she was doing it.

Just then, as if another unspoken prayer were being answered, Marshal Blake said, "Jenny, you couldn't make any sandwiches for us, could you? We're just stopping for a quick drink and to warm up, but we'll be heading out in a few minutes in hopes of pickin' up them long-loopers' trail down in the Porcupine Creek country. Too cold to ride far on empty bellies."

Jenny hadn't put together much of a free lunch plate today, as she'd figured business would be slow and she didn't have food to waste.

"Why, sure I can, Brian," Jenny said, almost leaping with a relieved start and again having to put her enthusiasm on a short leash. "I have a deer hangin' in the mudroom. Just let me go back and cut some loin meat off it, and I'll work you up some good venison sandwiches. How would that be?"

"That would be fine as frog hair, Miss Jenny!" said Sheriff Patten, running a big, gnarled red hand back through his wavy pewter hair.

"Be back in a few minutes!"

Jenny walked through a curtained doorway flanking the back bar and into the kitchen, which was dingy due to the light coming from only the single small window in the far wall. She did, indeed, have a deer hanging in the mudroom off the kitchen, but instead of heading for the mudroom, she began scrambling around for pencil and paper. Finding a stub of a pencil but no notepad, she ripped a corner off last month's calendar leaf, set it on the edge of the large black range, and touched the tip of the pencil to her tongue.

What should she write?

Several possibilities ran through her mind and then, knowing her time was limited, and with a heavily thudding heart and shaky fingers—she hoped that Patten could read her handwriting—she settled for simply: "The card players are wanted killers!" It took her nearly half a minute to scribble out the words, not wanting to misspell any of them and cause confusion.

She wanted to add that Patten should be careful, but he was the sheriff, for chrissakes, and she didn't have time to write anything else. The sheriff would know how careful he needed or didn't need to be. All Jenny could do was warn him about who the card players were and get them out of here. Hell, they might even be part of the rustling gang Patten and the federal men were after.

Jenny peered through a hole in the wall that looked out on the main drinking hall, just right of the Regulator clock. The three outlaws were still playing poker. The lawmen and the Double Bar T man were leaning against the bar, the three lawmen talking among themselves in a low, confidential monotone while the Double Bar T foreman simply leaned on his elbows, staring into the back bar mirror, smoothing down his mustache wet from melted frost.

Jenny gave a relieved sigh. All was still quiet.

She headed for the curtained doorway, the note clenched in her right fist.

As she pushed through it, before she was back behind the bar, she heard a familiar but vaguely threatening voice say, "Which direction did you boys ride in from?"

Jenny drew a sharp breath through gritted teeth and stopped just outside the kitchen, letting the curtain jostle back into place behind her. Patten no longer stood at the bar. He was standing over near the outlaws' table, holding the flaps of his big deer hide coat back behind his hips, looking down at the three men scowling up at him.

"Oh, no," Jenny muttered under her breath. "Oh, no, no, no . . ."

The two federals remained at the bar, leaning back against it, elbows on the edge of it. The Double Bar T foreman stood sideways to the bar, one elbow on it, a drink in one hand. He was facing Patten and the three outlaws.

Jenny could tell that neither Patten nor the two other lawmen nor the Double T foreman knew who the three outlaws were. Patten was just inquiring which direction they'd ridden in from because it had occurred to the sheriff that they might possibly be the rustlers that he and the federal men were looking for.

He didn't think there was much of a chance. Jenny could tell that. Because neither Patten nor any of the other men appeared ready for a fight.

Inside Jenny's head, a shrill voice screeched, "No, no, no. Sheriff, be careful!"

"What business is that of yours, mister?" asked Drake, wrinkling his nose until it resembled a pig's snout.

Patten didn't say anything. He just moved his left hand a little farther back behind his hip, pulling his coat flap back as well, showing the badge pinned to his flannel shirt.

"Oh, a lawman, huh?" said Drake, looking neither surprised nor impressed. He glanced at his two partners and then slid his chair back and pushed himself to his feet.

"Just stay seated," Patten ordered, gesturing with his hand.

Too late. Drake was already standing, his coat pulled back behind his six-shooters. Jenny was remembering how quickly he'd drawn one of those guns and blown the shot glass off the pyramid. Her heart hiccupped, lurched, hiccupped again. She felt her hands grow wet with sweat.

"Oh, no, no," Drake said with mock gravity. "I want to stand in honor of your presence here, sir."

Drake grinned, doffed his hat, and held it over his chest. Jenkins and McKirk did, as well.

One of the federal men pushed up from the bar and tensed. "Hey, that's Emory Drake!" He thrust out a pointing finger. As he did, the other federal man also tensed. Even the Double Bar T foreman must have recognized the name, because he lifted his elbow from the bar. From her vantage, Jenny could see that the left side of his face was suddenly losing its color.

Patten whipped a stricken look toward the federal man who'd identified Drake. Then, just as quickly, he turned back to Drake. The other two outlaws suddenly slid their own chairs back and rose, smirking. Jenny thought of a pair of rattlesnakes slowly winding themselves into attack-ready coils. They, too, had their coat flaps slid back behind their jutting pistols.

As brave and capable a man as Patten was, Jenny could see the fear stiffen his legs and shoulders. It made his ears—at least the one she could see from her angle near the curtained kitchen doorway—turn red. He took two slow steps back and said in a low, even voice, "All right, now . . . let's just everybody calm down."

"Oh, I'm calm, Sheriff." Drake glanced at his pards. "Ain't you boys calm?"

"Hell, I'm calm," said Jenkins.

"Yeah, me, too," allowed Vincent McKirk. "Hell, I'm as calm as a butterfly on a still day." He slid his eyes to the three men standing at the bar—the federals standing about two feet apart, the Double Bar T foreman standing a good ways beyond them, nearly right across the bar from Jenny. "What about you three fellas? You calm?"

None of those three said anything. They just stood tensely facing the three smirking outlaws. They looked as unnerved as jackrabbits who'd just found that they'd strolled unwittingly into a hole teeming with diamond-backs.

Patten glanced quickly at the two federals. The sheriff's eyes were opaque with tension. He seemed to be silently conferring with the two deputy marshals, but apparently the marshals gave Patten no signal. Jenny could almost hear the voices inside their heads scream-ing, "Oh, shit! Oh, shit! Oh, shit!"

Patten's right cheek twitched slightly. He turned back to the three smirking outlaws and said in his low, gravelly voice, "You three are gonna have to . . ." He paused to clear his throat. "You three are gonna have to set them pistols down . . . real easy-like . . . and come with us."

Drake laughed as casually as though he'd just heard

a joke told at a rodeo or a carnival. Neither he nor his cohorts looked one bit nervous. In fact, they appeared to be thoroughly enjoying the confrontation. Drake was still holding his hat over his heart, but now he set it back down on his head as he said, "You can't be fool enough to think that's really gonna happen, Sheriff. No, no— *that* ain't gonna happen. But you know what *is* gonna happen?"

"What's that?" Patten asked, dreadfully.

Vincent McKirk answered for Drake, his voice suddenly soft and menacing. "You four are gonna die."

The Double Bar T foreman raised his hands to shoulder height and said suddenly, "Hey, I got no part in this, Drake! I ain't a lawman. I'm from the Double Bar T, and I was just showin' these *here* lawmen the tracks of some cows that got rustled!"

Drake laughed again. "Well, all right, then. Don't just stand there pissin' down your leg, you tinhorned coward! Get outta here now! Run back to your ranch and tell the other hands what a big man you was here today, facin' down Emory Drake, Curly Jenkins, and Vincent McKirk!"

As the Double Bar T foreman turned and ran to the front door, which he nearly tore off its hinges before he finally got outside, Drake and the others laughed uproariously.

Patten must have thought they were sufficiently distracted. Jenny's heart leaped into her throat when she saw his right elbow jerk. It was hard to tell from her position, but she didn't think that the county sheriff had even gotten his revolver halfway out of its holster before

Drake and his two partners had their own guns out and up and started blasting away.

Jenny screamed when she saw blood spewing out Sheriff Patten's back as the killers' bullets tore through him. Then the other two lawmen were screaming and jerking, though Jenny saw nothing more of the slaughter because she dropped to her hands and knees behind the bar, her own screams drowned by the cacophony of the gunfire.

The reports sounded like the thunder of cannon in the close confines of the barroom. They continued for so long that Jenny had to stick her fingers in her ears to keep her drums from rupturing. It sounded as though Patten or the other two lawmen were returning fire. She could hear several men shouting high-pitched curses. Boots hammered the wooden floor on the other side of the bar, spurs ringing loudly.

After what seemed like a long Dakota winter but was probably only about two minutes, a face appeared over the top of the bar, staring down at Jenny. Jenny screamed with a start. Then she saw that the face, blood-splattered and bright-eyed with fear and agony, his pewter hair hanging down over his forehead, belonged to Sheriff Patten.

Patten lurched and squeezed his eyes closed as a bullet tore into him from behind.

"Jenny!" he groaned beneath the continuing din, gritting his teeth. "Telegraph office! Send . . . to . . . Marshal . . . Billy Vail . . . in . . . Denver! Have him"—he jerked again, screaming—"have him send *Longarm!*"

Then his eyes fluttered closed, his head hit the top of the bar, and he slid back down the other side and out of sight.

As the guns continued roaring behind her, Jenny crawled through the curtain into the kitchen and then ran out the saloon's side door, sobbing and muttering, "*Longarm!*"

Chapter 3

"Such a cold winter night," the girl said, shivering. "Makes me wish I was all curled up in a bear rug in front of a hot fire with a glass or two of good brandy or hot spiced wine. It is Christmas Eve, after all. We really should be holed up somewhere warm—don't you think, Marshal Long?"

"You mean, holed up somewhere *together*, Miss Johnson?" inquired Deputy U.S. Marshal Custis P. Long, known far and wide by friend and foe as Longarm.

The tall, broad-shouldered lawman's dark brown mustache, known as a longhorn due its upswept ends, both spread and rose in a wolfish grin. His dark brown eyes glittered in the flickering light of the several lanterns bracketed to the walls of the rocking, clacking coach car, which was part of a twelve-car combination making its slow, cold way across the snowy Dakota Territory plain mantled this chilly December evening by crisp, clear stars sparkling like Christmas candles limning the firmament.

The girl tittered behind her hand and then reprimanded him with a sidelong, none-too-serious glare. "Oh, don't be silly, Marshal Long! I would never be so bold! I am a teacher, after all. Think of the poor children! Or . . . I will be a teacher, I mean. Once I arrive in Billings out in that cold and lonely place called Montana."

The girl, who couldn't have been much over seventeen, glanced at the dark, soot-stained window through which the rolling, snow-covered plain could vaguely be seen, though it mostly reflected the guttering light of the smoky oil lamps. It was like she was looking out at a land called Forever locked under a blanket of snow and subzero temperatures, and the idea of her residing there chilled her to the bone.

"And, anyway, even if I wasn't a teacher, that is not the way I was raised, Marshal Long," she said, turning away from the bleak scene out the dark window and favoring Longarm with a more pleasant, slightly coquettish gaze, her lustrous, light brown eyes crossing slightly.

Miss Mathilda Johnson was a honey-blonde with wide, clean cheekbones, honest eyes, and a spray of freckles across her straight, frank nose, bespeaking a Midwestern farm girl. And that's what she'd told Longarm she indeed was when they'd first started talking a half hour ago, just as the train had been pulling out of the little Dakota river settlement of Grand Forks along the Red River of the North. She'd been raised outside the little Minnesota farming town of Leafy

Knoll, "on a dairy farm, though my father also raised wheat and corn but mostly for the cows," and that she was "going to miss Ma and Pa and dear little Johnny and sweet Mary Beth so much I'm already having trouble catching my breath."

But she'd gone to teaching school back East, and upon her recent graduation—"with honors, I might add"—she'd answered an ad from a little place in eastern Montana that needed a teacher. The school board had responded to her query in only two weeks, asking her to come right away as the former schoolmaster had died of a heart stroke and they needed a new teacher in place right after New Year's. So here the poor girl was, traveling on Christmas to some canker on the devil's ass (Longarm's unvoiced words, not hers) on a cold, drafty, smelly, half-empty train and chatting with a weary federal marshal who hated nothing so much as the northern prairie after, say, August 15 because of the possibility of snow.

Longarm hated snow.

But here he was, having just finished one job running owlhoots to bay in the snow up near the Canadian border. He'd intended to be back in Denver by Christmas and spend the holidays frolicking naked with his comely pal Cynthia Larimer, but the lawman's previous assignment had taken longer—and been more grueling—than expected.

And before boarding the train in Grand Forks, he'd received a telegram from his boss, Chief Marshal Billy Vail of the First District Federal Court of Colorao in Denver, informing him that his services were needed pronto in Little Missouri City, Dakota Territory, to investigate the killings of several lawmen. Chief Vail's message had been brief, but he'd mentioned that three killers had murdered a couple of deputy U.S. marshals and a local lawman; that's why the whole nasty business had fallen into Longarm's snow-and-cold-hating, Cynthia-missing, ungrateful lap.

Longarm had traveled through Little Missouri City on his trip to Minnesota, and he'd had a drink with the county sheriff out that way, Sheriff Lew Patten. Longarm hoped the killings hadn't involved Patten, a good man and longtime friend of the federal badge-toter.

"My dear Miss Johnson," Longarm said, "what on earth does how you were or were not raised have to do with staying warm on a cold and lonely Christmas Eve?" He hiked a shoulder. "Sounds like mere survival to me."

The girl tittered and the nubs of her peaches-and-cream cheeks flushed crimson. "I guess that's one way of looking at it."

"And I didn't necessarily mean 'together' in the Biblical sense. It just so happens I have a sleeping compartment back in the Pullman car. I slipped the porter a few extra coins to make sure the compartment, the largest one in the sleeping coach, was appointed with its own small but mightily effective woodstove."

Longarm glanced over his right shoulder at the sheet-iron stove sitting hunched near the coach's rear wall. "That one there doesn't seem very effective."

The lawman did not have to feign a bone-rattling shiver, for it was truly cold in the passenger coach. The dozen or so other pilgrims—a few drummers and a couple of sullen-looking soldiers but mostly raggedy-heeled saddle tramps finding themselves both unemployed and in transit on Christmas—sat hunched deep in their coats, occasionally stomping their feet and shivering. A couple were reading newspapers but mostly it was too cold to do much of anything except concentrate on trying to evade frostbite.

The stove was obviously too small, and the wood the porter occasionally fed it too green, to hold the subzero cold of the plains winter night at bay.

"No, it certainly doesn't," said Mathilda Johnson, burying her chin in the wide collar of her ratty buffalo coat. The coat was too bulky to give an indication of the girl's build, but something told Longarm she was a farm girl in full flower. And the frankness of her eyes belied the timidity of her personality.

He had a feeling the girl had a lusty nature. Miss Mathilda had probably even given her virginity to a boy from a neighboring farm or maybe a seasonal field worker. What curious young farm boy or girl hadn't been tempted to try what the heifers and bulls and the mares and stallions were always doing without chagrin?

On the other hand, the girl from Leafy Knoll might truly be as pure as the fresh Dakota snow piled into wave-shaped drifts along the tracks. If that turned out to be the case, Longarm had no intention of being her first. That should be left to someone not only closer to her own age, but one who wouldn't be giving her a good-day pinch of his hat brim the following morning.

Longarm was a letch, to be sure. But he was a letch not entirely without scruples.

The girl continued with, "That does sound sorta good. I don't reckon Ma or Pa or Johnny or sweet Mary

Beth would mind if I didn't freeze to death." She gave
Longarm a critical, sidelong look. "You aren't a Mister
Baddie—are you, Marshal Long?"

"A Mister Baddie?"

"Yeah, you know," Miss Mathilda said. "A lusty mister who just wants to strip all a girl's clothes off her body
and grunt around on top of her, sticking his stiff rod
between her legs and sucking her titties?" She snickered
a little too loudly and heartily and then jerked a frightened look around the car, wondering if any of the other
passengers had heard.

Longarm shifted uncomfortably in his seat and said,
"Well, now, Miss Johnson, I can assure you that . . ."

"You look like a lusty devil, Marshal Long," the girl
said when she'd satisfied herself that the other passengers were too busy trying not to freeze to death to eaves-
drop on her conversation with Longarm. She blinked
slowly and nibbled her thumbnail with a speculative air.
"Is that true?"

Longarm somehow managed to keep a straight face.
"Miss Johnson, I assure you that your honor is safe
with me."

"Well, in that case, I reckon you might as well call
me Mattie . . . since I'm gonna be sharing your sleeping
compartment and all, Marshal Long."

Longarm was rocked back in his seat with surprise.
And, for some reason, he felt a bit guilty. Well, he knew
the reason for his guilt. His intentions had not been
all that innocent. Perhaps that was why he was so surprised that the girl was taking him up on his offer when
all he'd actually been doing was playing the habitual
flirt.

Now that she had taken him up on the invitation, he remonstrated himself, he would have to act the perfect gentleman. Which meant that he'd probably be sleeping on the Pullman's cold floor, giving young Miss Mattie his bed. If he remembered correctly from when he'd walked through the car earlier, the floor had been bare, uncarpeted wood. Likely damn near as cold as the steel rails the train's iron wheels were clacking over at this very moment.

Perhaps he'd just played one hell of a prank on himself. If so, it would serve him right.

"What's the matter, Marshal Long?" the girl asked him, leaning forward and looking concerned. "Don't you feel well?"

"No, no, I'm fine, Miss Mattie. And . . . uh . . . since I reckon we'll be sharing my Pullman compartment, you might as well call me Longarm. Most folks do—at least them who know me well enough to share a sleeper!"

He chuckled and rose from his hard, cold, velour-covered seat, stepped into the aisle, and grabbed his sheathed rifle from the overhead rack.

"My, that's a big gun," the girl remarked and stepped out into the aisle, jerking and pulling a large carpetbag, which had been residing in the seat beside her. She'd told Longarm the grip was filled with needlework, which she'd intended to do on the train to pass the time.

Longarm took her bag from her, gestured for her to go ahead of him, and ten minutes later, after a long, cold walk through two other mostly empty coach cars, they passed through the tooth-splintering wind and blowing snow of one last observation platform and entered his sleeping compartment, which the porter had freshly prepared. The compartment was toasty warm, the small woodstove, a little larger than a footlocker, ticking and crackling. The glow of the fire shone through the crack around the door. The bed had been made up, a thick quilt and wool blanket pulled back to reveal snowy cotton sheets and a pillow.

"Here we are, Miss Mattie—home sweet home. I'll just step outside and enjoy my pre-slumberin' cigar while you make yourself comfortable. The compartment's too small for us to both be stumblin' around in it together."

"Oh, you won't be gone long, will you, Marshal Lo— I mean, Longarm?" the girl said, placing a hand on his forearm and squeezing. "Suddenly . . . with all the strange men aboard the train, many of whom have been giving me typically seedy looks . . . I'm a bit frightened. I'm so glad you're here!"

She squeezed his forearm a little tighter. He had seen a couple of the men in the coach car pass her fleeting, depraved looks, so he could understand her worry.

Longarm smiled down at her and patted her hand that still gripped his forearm. "I'll be right outside there, Miss Mattie, blowin' my smoke out the door. You just go ahead and do whatever you have to do to get comfortable, and I'll be back shortly to throw down on the floor."

He sort of muttered that last under his breath as he set her carpetbag down on the bed, leaned his rifle in a corner, and headed back outside.

He took his time smoking the cigar and blowing the smoke out the cracked front vestibule door. While he was glad that the girl would have a warm place to sleep, he also castigated himself for letting his trouser snake cause him a hard night's sleep on a cold floor on a train rocking through the high, frozen plains of Dakota.

"Fool," he said, taking a deep drag off one of his beloved three-for-a-nickel cheroots, rocking from side to side with the sway of the train. "Tin-plated, copper-riveted fool . . ."

Ten minutes later, he knocked on the door and said softly, "Miss Mattie?"

"Yes, come in, Longarm."

He went inside and felt his heart turn a somersault.

The girl stood before him wearing only a slit-eyed smile.

Chapter 4

"What's the matter, Longarm?" the girl asked in a sexy-raspy voice, standing before him and cupping her bare breasts in her hands. "Cat got your tongue?"

Longarm glanced both ways along the Pullman's central aisle lit by only two bracket lamps, one of which had nearly gone out in the cold draft sweeping from one end of the car to the other. Seeing no one else out and about, he stepped quickly into his and the girl's compartment and drew the door closed behind him.

"Miss . . . uh . . . I mean . . . uh . . . Mattie—you don't have a stitch on, girl!"

He knew he sounded like a six-year-old boy who'd just spied his big sis in her birthday suit, but the unexpectedness of seeing her naked—not to mention how perfect her body was!—had tied his brain as well as his tongue in knots.

"How good of you to notice, Longarm."

She swung her hips as she walked to him and hooked

first one arm and then the other around his neck, rising up on her bare toes to get the top of her head even with his chin.

"I hope I'm not being brash. It's just that I couldn't help enjoying how you were dining on me with your eyes earlier, and how safe and warm and how much like a woman you were making me feel. You see, I've always been bothered by a rather healthy but pesky appetite for fucking."

Mattie stretched her pink lips back from her small white teeth in a foxy grin. "At least, since I was old enough to start enjoying it, if you get my drift. I was raised on a farm, and, well, after watching the dogs and horses doing it, I couldn't help but feel a little randy after a while. So when Clifton Wallace, the boy who cut and hauled firewood for my pa, caught me playing with myself in the barn one cold winter day and showed me his dong . . . well, I've been gone for stiff dongs ever since!"

"Holy shit," Longarm muttered, reflecting that he'd been right, after all.

Farm girls!

Seeing her lifting up still farther on her bare toes and tipping her head back, thrusting her ripe mouth toward his, he couldn't help but doff his hat and gather her in.

Soon he had her tightly ensconced in his arms and they were tongue wrestling deep inside one's and then the other's mouth. Mattie groaned in his embrace, pressing her thighs against his and wriggling against him until his cock was so hard he was afraid it would tear through his winter-weight, fleece-lined balbriggans as well as his brown tweed trousers.

She must have felt his cock push against her belly. She gave a thrilled mewl and dropped one of her small, warm hands to massage him through his pants.

"Oh, my God!" she wheezed, looking down. "Is that as big as it feels?"

Longarm tried to get ahold of himself. He stepped back against the door. She was awfully young and he was beginning to think she might be overly vulnerable, heading out so far from home on a toe-curlingly cold winter evening. Christmas Eve, no less!

As warm as his blood was, he didn't want to take advantage of her. Hell, she most likely wasn't even twenty years old . . .

"Miss Mattie, let's rein up a mite, shall we?"

"Shhh!" She grinned up at him from beneath her honey-blond brows, smiling beguilingly, and then slowly sank down to her knees. Her fingers moved rather adroitly over his fly buttons, as though she were not unaccustomed to the maneuver, and in less time than it took him to draw two deep breaths, rocking back on the heels of his cavalry stovepipes, she had his fly open and was reaching inside.

Once inside his trousers, she waggled her hand through the fly of his heavy balbriggans and curved her fingers around his fully erect cock. She slowly squeezed, as though he were the neck of a rooster she were about to make ready for the stewpot.

"Holy jeepers!" she said, giggling and then pulling the thick, heavy snake out of its hole.

Longarm groaned through gritted teeth as she leaned her head forward and touched the tip of her tongue to the head of his cock and then drew it away quickly.

"You like that?"

Longarm only groaned.

She giggled delightedly, then closed her eyes and bathed the whole swollen head of his dick with the tip of her small pink tongue.

Longarm decided to go ahead and surrender to the girl's charms. She was obviously no virgin. Not even a beginner. The way she continued to lick and gently pump his raging hard-on with both hands told him that she was a journeyman on the fast trail to being an expert with a fully rounded-out reputation. Vaguely, he wondered about her being a teacher with such a surging sexual appetite when she'd no doubt be teaching at least a handful of boys. And then he heard himself giving a soft, amused snort at the prospect.

Those young Montana honyockers were likely going to learn a hell of a lot more than how to read and cypher, and Longarm had a feeling they weren't going to be too disappointed in the extracurricular learning that would likely take place in the cloak-and-galoshes room after regular school hours.

When she'd brought him dangerously close to climax, he placed his hands on her shoulders and gently lifted her to a standing position before him. She licked her upper lip and ran the back of her hand across her mouth, smiling lustily.

"Mmm," she said. "Can't take it anymore, Longarm?"

"Nope."

Longarm kicked off his boots and then shucked out of his clothes as fast as he could, staggering drunkenly with the swaying Pullman. Naked, cock jutting, he walked up to her. She stepped back, wrapped one hand around his hard-on, and sat down on the edge of the bed. She spread her legs impossibly wide, and her pink mound of Venus opened, glistening in the light of the bracket lamp.

She shook her hair back from flushed cheeks.

She groaned like a dog in heat as he bent over her, and she used her hand to guide his cock into the sweet, succulent folds of her warm, wet snatch. He thrust his hips forward but stopped when she said, "Oh—*ow!*"

"All right?" he asked her.

She nodded, gritting her teeth and looking down at his shaft, half of which was inside her. "It's so big!"

"We can stop."

"Don't you dare!"

She laughed huskily as she wrapped her hands around his thighs and drew him down slowly, incrementally sliding his cock into her. He could feel her pussy expanding and contracting around his shaft, clutching him, the juices oozing around him, making for easier and easier going.

Then he was so deep inside her he thought he could feel one of her ribs nestled up against the swollen head of his penis.

"Oh," she said, throwing her head back, silky blond hair hanging straight down toward the bed. "Oh, oh! You . . . feel . . . *soo* . . . good!"

Longarm rammed his hips against her slowly at first, taking about five seconds to drive his shaft all the way in and then another five to pull it nearly all the way out, until only the very tip was keeping the folds of her flower open. Then he began the torturous maneuver all over again. He kept up this pace, causing her to mewl

and grit her teeth and drive her heels into the backs of
his thighs, for about five minutes.

Meanwhile, the train rocked and swayed and he could
feel the cold pushing through the window in front of
him while the stove bathed his naked ass and legs with
its dry, crisp, gradually diminishing heat.

Before him, despite the cold behind her, a fine sheen
of sweat rose on Mattie's firm, peach-colored breasts.
Their nipples were fully erect and jutting slightly to each
side, the enticing orbs themselves jostling as Longarm
continued to toil between her spread knees. Sometimes
she pushed off her elbows to reach around him and dig
her fingernails into his ass. The pain was so bittersweet
that it drove shafts of delight down his legs and, on two
occasions, nearly caused him to come way ahead of
time.

"Faster," Mattie groaned after they'd been going at
it for about ten minutes, Longarm having only doubled
his speed in the last five. "Oh, faster! Please, Longarm.
Oh, God . . . you're fucking killing me . . . !"

"No," he snarled, though the pulsating heart of passion pumping away inside his balls was calling for the
same thing that Mattie was.

But he knew that to arrive at optimum pleasure for
both himself and the girl, he had to keep himself on a
semitight rein.

Mattie sobbed in bittersweet anguish as she looked
down past her bouncing tits and her rapidly expanding
and contracting belly to the thick, long cock sliding in
and out of her, the foreskin appearing ahead of the swollen mushroom head itself before drawing taut along the
shaft as he drove himself inside her once more.

The flickering lamplight bathed the slick shaft in crimson light. It bathed Mattie's sopping pussy, too, and shone briefly in the droplets of her hot oozings sliding down Longarm's legs to the floor.

Suddenly, after he'd been fucking the poor girl for twenty minutes, Longarm stopped. She'd been lying flat on the bed for the past six minutes or so, arms thrown out to both sides and turning her head to one side as he'd pushed into her and then to the other side when he'd started pulling out. Longarm held the head of his cock against the outside of her hot snatch, gritting his teeth and willing his blood to cool down enough so he could continue fucking her without blowing his load.

But then he felt her vagina begin to quiver. It was like an earth tremor building toward an all-out quake.

Longarm could have sworn he heard the low rumble of distant seas. Mattie lifted her head from the bed to cast him the keenest look of desperate beseeching he thought he'd ever seen on anyone's face in any circumstance. He reached forward and clamped a hand over the girl's open mouth, muffling her scream lest she alarm the entire car, though he thought there might only be three or four other people occupying the Pullman.

At the same time, her pussy grabbed at him and grew hotter.

"Ah, shit!" Longarm rasped.

Her cunt's fierce grabbing busted through the dam of his passion like sixty tons of dynamite. He thrust his hips forward, ramming himself deep inside her. He pulled out quickly, thrust forward with a savage grunt. Mattie screamed into his hand, and he could feel her hot breath and saliva against his palm as her cunt clutched him double hard, spasming and oozing as she came.

Longarm came then, too, as he continued ramming himself in and out of her, driving her head up to the outside wall of the Pullman before he pulled her back toward him and continued thrusting himself in and out of her.

His cock spurted jets of jism like a Gatling gun throwing .45-caliber chunks of lead at a shitload of attacking Comanche warriors. The girl was rigid and quivering beneath him, mewling and sobbing into his palm as he came deep inside her and she came against him.

Finally, they both relaxed upon the bed. Longarm rolled to one side. The girl was limp as a rag. He slid his arms under her and arranged her on the bed beside him. Then he lay back, relaxing.

"Whew!" he said, chest rising and falling as he tried to catch his breath.

"That was wonderful," she said in a high, trembling voice through a ragged sigh.

Longarm swallowed, gave a sigh of his own. "Yeah . . ."

"I'm so sorry, Longarm."

He'd closed his eyes. Now he opened them. She was leaning over him, sweaty, chafed breasts slanting toward his chest. Her wide eyes were liquid with anguish.

"What's that?" he said.

But then she threw her arm back behind her shoulder a quarter second before gritting her teeth and slamming something hard down against his head. It must have been a rock or something just as hard.

The speculation was his last, half-formed thought before the world became a dark and painful place.

Mattie cleaned up a bit and got dressed.

Then she opened the sleeping compartment door, looking down toward the car's far end, and beckoned. "All clear, Reverend!" she called.

Chapter 5

They called Horace Clancy "the Reverend," but he was about as pious as an Apache holding an innocent settler's dripping heart in one hand, a bloody butcher knife in the other, and thrusting both above his head, whooping and hollering while he danced around his victim's corpse.

The Reverend was a tall, whipcord-thin, dark-haired, blue-eyed Tennessee dandy sporting a dark suit and a minister's collar beneath an ankle-length fox fur coat that had seen much better days. As the Reverend limped into the sleeping compartment—the Dakota chill was giving his gimpy left ankle fits—he shoved his black slouch hat back off his pale forehead and grinned at the girl, who was on one knee, going through Longarm's pants pockets.

"Well, now, Missy Mattie," the Reverend said in his petal-soft Southern accent, "wasn't you havin' *fun?* Why, this hombre's hung like a Tennessee mule!"

The girl who was at the moment calling herself Mattie Johnson but whose traveling acting troupe parents had named her Miss Arlis Watson when she'd been born nineteen years ago in a covered wagon outside the Colorado mountain mining town of Creede, snapped an anxious look at the tall, mild-eyed Tennessean with whom she'd been running confidence scams across the West for the past three years.

"No one heard, did they?" she asked the Reverend.

"Heard what?"

"Heard me scream! Christ almighty, Reverend, I've never been plundered like that in all my days. He liked to have snapped me like a wishbone!"

The Reverend snorted as he turned to look up and down the hall. Seeing no one around, he closed the sleeping compartment door behind him. He kept his voice low as he dug into a pocket of his coat for a flat brown bottle and popped the cork from the lip. "I didn't hear anything, my cherub. I was smoking down at the other end of the car. Screamed rather loudly, did you, while this hombre was . . . uh . . . molesting you, you poor child?"

The Reverend tipped back the bourbon bottle.

Mattie snickered. One of her and the Reverend's frequent scams was to accuse an upstanding citizen of whatever town they were working in of rape, or of attempted rape. Only after Mattie seduced the gent, of course. Then she and the Reverend threatened to report the "vile, no-account, child-molesting pervert," whose dick was still wet, to the nearest authorities unless their befuddled and horrified quarry forked over a good-sized lump of scrip and specie.

The Reverend's part in the scam was to play the innocent Miss Mattie's traveling preacher brother, the Reverend Richmond C. Turnbull, who often held church services in a circus tent of whatever town they were scamming. The Reverend was such a good actor and orator that his shows often left grown men teary-eyed and dumping fistfuls of money into the hat that somber-faced Mattie passed around in a low-cut black frock, which strategically exposed a goodly portion of her creamy cleavage.

"Damn," Mattie said, pulling a slender sheaf of bills from the wallet she'd been plundering. "Must be less than twenty-five dollars here."

The Reverend returned the flask to his coat pocket and knelt to help the girl go through her most recent victim's strewn clothes, looking for valuables. "Can't be," the Reverend said. "He's a gambler—I know he is. The three-piece suit and string tie was a dead giveaway. He's got to have more money than that on him. Have you looked for a money belt?"

"Reverend?" Mattie said.

He looked at her, frowning. "What is it?"

"He's a lawman." Mattie held up the star-and-moon badge that had been pinned to the inside of Longarm's wallet. The pretty girl had turned her mouth corners down.

"Good God!" exclaimed the Reverend, cupping a black-gloved hand to his mouth in astonishment. "When did you find that out?"

"Back in the coach car. But . . ." Mattie shrugged with chagrin and looked over at the big, naked, well-hung gent sprawled on his back across the bed, blood trickling from the deep gash in his left temple. "I don't know . . . he seemed so nice and friendly. And he was such a big, handsome cuss that . . . I don't know . . . I decided to let him fuck me, figurin' it had to be worth at least a *few* dollars."

"Oh, dear. Oh, dear." The Reverend doffed his hat and held it over his heart as he peered down at the lawman. "Is he dead?"

"I don't think so," Mattie said, stuffing the money from Longarm's wallet into a pocket of her coat.

"Well, he will be soon," said the Reverend, pulling a long, black-handled folding knife out of his fox fur coat.

As he opened the long, wickedly slender blade, Mattie placed a hand on the Reverend's wrist. "Oh, Reverend, no!"

The Reverend looked at her, frowning. "But, Mattie, he *must* die, or you and I will . . . !"

He let his voice trail off as he studied the girl's beseeching eyes, as she dug her fingers into his wrist.

"Oh, I see," the Reverend said with gentle understanding. "This one became a little more than a mark, didn't he, dear Mattie?"

"I don't know," the girl said, looking down at the big man sound asleep on the bed, big dick slumped to one side. Longarm's cock was still glistening with his and Mattie's oozings. "I reckon maybe he did. Sort of."

The Reverend chuckled and put away his knife. "Well, I reckon I can see why! All right, then. I won't cut him. But you know what must be done."

Mattie turned her mouth corners down again as she said, "Yeah, I know."

"Do you think we can do it together?" The Reverend sighed. "Awfully big man . . . in more ways than one!" He wheezed another laugh as he popped the cork on his bourbon bottle and threw back another couple of large swallows.

"Yeah, we can do it. Beats makin' a big mess an' all," Mattie said. "I heard him talkin' to the porter earlier. Sounds like they're friends. If the porter comes callin' and finds this big drink of water dead, he'll likely stop the train at the next town. If he just finds the compartment empty, it'll take him a while to figure out what happened. We'd best be long gone from here when Longarm's body's found, Reverend."

"Indeed." The Reverend had crouched to curl his forearms under Longarm's armpits. "Help me, here, dearie!"

Mattie grabbed Longarm's ankles and she and the Reverend had a miserable time dragging the unconscious man out the compartment door and into the narrow hall. As they maneuvered, breathing hard and grunting with the effort, they strained to be as quiet as possible.

Still, there was much thumping as they half dragged and half carried the big man's heavy body down the aisle between compartments, through the door, and out onto the platform, after Mattie had first made sure no one was out on the platform smoking or, as she had witnessed a time or two, fucking.

But it was much too cold for anything like that, she was somewhat relieved to find.

When they'd gotten the big lawman onto the platform and sort of curled him into a fetal position, he started groaning and cursing, wagging his head. The cold had awakened him, as, no doubt, had the icy feel of the wood platform under him.

"Oh, dear," the Reverend said, "he's coming around!"

Quickly, he and Mattie got behind Longarm, crouched low, and shoved the naked man off the platform and into the windy, snowy darkness. Longarm's body briefly reflected the light from the windows of the coach car and then, arcing down toward the snowy ditch beyond the train, disappeared.

"Come, dearie," the Reverend said, beckoning. "We must scour every scrap of your donkey-dicked true love from the compartment!"

With Mattie on his heels, the tall, thin man in the clerical collar and fox fur coat returned to Longarm's sleeping compartment, gathered up the lawman's clothes and guns and hurled them off the platform into the snowy, windy night. The Reverend went back for the man's saddle, which sat on the floor in a corner of the compartment, and gave that the same treatment, as Mattie did with the man's saddlebags and bedroll.

"There!" the Reverend said, his long black hair blowing out behind him in the wind as he stood shivering and staring out into the night toward the rear of the train, in the direction they'd hurled the lawman to a surefire cold and snowy death. "It's done! Now, let that be a lesson to you, dearie. No more—!"

"I know," Mattie yelled above the thunder of the train and the wind. "No more lawmen! No matter how well they're hung!"

They chuckled seedily and then Mattie returned to the coach car in which she'd been riding earlier with

Longarm, and the Reverend repaired to the club car. He was in dire need of some hot coffee into which he could dump his bourbon.

The pillowy drift of new-fallen snow closed around Longarm like a wave of the coldest ocean anywhere in the universe. Instantly, before he'd even stopped rolling through the frigid stuff, he was awake, heart leaping into his throat and turning somersaults.

Every nerve was frightfully alive. He heard himself grunting and gasping as he continued being hurled through the drifts piled up along the side of the track bed as though by an unseen hand. His head throbbed and his ears rang. But those were minor complaints compared to the frozen ocean that had wrapped itself around him like an all-encompassing blanket.

When he finally stopped rolling, he found himself lying spread-eagle on his back, staring up at the sky in which tiny stars shone weakly in gaps between gauzy clouds. Snow stitched the air around him—large, fuzzy flakes. For a minute, he felt as though he were burning. But then the burning turned back into a bone-splintering chill.

He lifted his head, looking around. The world danced around him. His brains were so scrambled that he could not get an immediate handle on what had just happened or even where in the hell he was. But then the words "snow" and "cold" and "alone" and "naked" and "Dakota" found themselves through the misty cavern of his consciousness. And then the misty memory of being dragged through the Pullman's central aisle and out onto the front platform also clarified.

He gave a great gasp, sucking air into his lungs and wrapping himself in his brawny arms, shivering and shuddering and loudly groaning as he stared off west down the railroad bed, where the train from which he had been so unceremoniously removed was a weak, fast-diminishing red light.

"Shit!" he raked out, though anyone listening would have found the word unintelligible for the clattering of his teeth.

The snow and the air were so cold that he was already numb. He couldn't feel his hands or his toes. But he scrambled madly up out of the drift and crawled through the heavy powder toward the tracks.

The rail bed was steep and covered in two feet of snow in places. He slipped and slid, unable to gain purchase. He cursed as he rolled back down the slope to the mussed snow at the bottom. But then he was up again, gasping as though he were drowning in a frozen sea, and continued to madly scramble, dragging his cock and balls through the snow.

The rails were the only sign of life out here. There was nothing else except the black night relieved solely by the paleness of the snow that was everywhere.

And more was coming down.

In the back of his cold and pain-fogged mind, the thought clung that the rails were his only hope of salvation, as though by reaching them he were somehow reaching the train, though that couldn't possibly be so. The train was gone. Not even the weak amber light from the train windows remained over the rails to the west. There was only the gauzy darkness stitched with large, fuzzy flakes of falling snow.

Longarm stared off down the tracks—a haunted man.

Only darkness there. Above, falling snow and the stars that were too dim even to twinkle.

On all fours, he turned his head, looking around himself in a full circle. He could see nothing but the vague undulations of the prairie beneath its heavy ermine coat. He turned onto his butt and hugged himself, shivering. His entire body was numbing. It was as though a powerful drug had been injected into his feet and hands. It was working its way through his bloodstream, turning each muscle to stone.

"Can't stay here," he said, though everything in him wanted to give up and go to sleep. "Can't stay. Gotta . . . gotta move . . . until I can't move . . . no more . . ."

Longarm got up and began running blindly along the side of the tracks. He had no idea which direction to head, so he decided to head in the same direction as the train. Eventually, he would reach a settlement. Maybe not for many yards, possibly not for many miles. But it was as good a direction as any.

And he had nothing else to do—except lie down and die.

He ran for maybe twenty yards. And then his numb feet stopped working, as did his numb legs, his numb knees. His numb brain. He fell and then rolled down the slope to pile up in a large, downy pillow of snow to sleep that last, long cold sleep in the chilly palm of the cosmos' massive hand.

Chapter 6

Longarm had just gone to sleep when there grew around him the low crunching sound of snow under heavy boots. Two figures appeared out of the snowy darkness to stand atop the rail bed, staring down at the naked man who was all but covered with snow. One of the figures was tall and wide and wrapped in a heavy fur cap and fur coat. The other, smaller figure was similarly attired.

The larger figure pointed at something along the side of the tracks, west of Longarm. While the smaller figure went running off up the tracks and then into the ditch beside it, the larger figure slipped and slid down the side of the rail bed. The larger figure stooped and lifted the naked, unconscious man over his right shoulder and then climbed the bank again, slipping and falling to a knee several times.

Finally gaining the crest of the rail bed, the larger figure carried Longarm west along the tracks to where a wagon waited, straddling the tracks themselves. As the large figure gentled the lawman into the wagon box and drew several fur robes and blankets over him, the smaller figure scurried out of the darkness with arms full of the clothes just retrieved from the snow along the tracks.

The larger and smaller figures conversed briefly with hand gestures, and then they both marched off up the tracks and into the snow at the side of the rail bed until they'd gathered up the rest of Longarm's belongings, including his hat and saddle, and had set them all in the wagon box beside the slumbering federal lawman. Then they each climbed up onto the driver's seat.

The larger figure released the brake and shook the reins over the back of the shaggy, beefy Percheron in the traces, and the wagon jerked and clattered on across the tracks and along a trail angling to the south, which appeared only now and then where the wind had cleared the snow.

Meanwhile, the lawman slept, shuddering, teeth clattering, in his sleep.

Longarm was awakened by the touch of warmth on his eyelids and his cheeks. The backs of his eyelids were orange, and when he opened his eyes, he saw that crystalline sunlight was angling through a window of the room he was in. The light spread two long rectangles across the star quilt covering him—one wide rectangle, one slightly narrower. He could hear water splashing. He opened his eyes wider, blinked several times against the bright light. When his eyes adjusted, he found himself staring at the slender, bare back of a girl or a young woman.

He blinked again, lifted his head slightly from his pillow, and shook his head as though to clear his vision. Obviously, he was dreaming. But, no, the longer he kept his eyes on the girl's slender back, the more convinced he became that she was, in fact, real.

The girl stood about ten feet from the end of his bed, facing a wall against which stood a washstand and a porcelain bowl. She wore a simple cotton dress. She'd pulled the sleeves of her dress down to her waist, leaving her back bare to the bell-like flare of her hips and the top of her butt crack—and was slowly massaging her breasts with a sponge. Longarm could see the outside curves of both breasts as she jostled them, washing them, as well as part of the yellow sponge.

While she washed, she stood straight, head tipped slightly back and sort of lolling, as though she were thoroughly enjoying the caress of the wet, soapy sponge on her body. Long, chestnut hair hung straight down to the middle of her back, sliding this way and that as she bathed herself. Her incredibly smooth skin appeared suntanned, but Longarm figured it was her natural skin tone. Girls didn't expose themselves overmuch to the sun this time of year in Dakota.

The wood-framed windows to each side of her, across which flour sack curtains had been drawn, were bedecked with silver Christmas tinsel that twinkled like diamonds in the sunlight. In the corner of the room to her right was a spindly little ponderosa pine Christmas tree trimmed with more tinsel as well as with small red and white candles. It was topped by an ornament of scrolled brass wrapped in green and red felt and decorated with small white beads. Some kind of Old Country trimming, possibly Russian, the lawman silently opined.

He didn't give it too much thought, however. When he'd taken a quick scan of the rest of his surroundings, deciding that he was in a small, earthen-floored, sod-roofed settler's shack somewhere out on the Great Snowy Plains east of Little Missouri City, he returned his attention to the girl, who was continuing to give herself a whore's bath right in front of him, though he was relatively certain she was no whore. As he admired the view, he took stock of himself and his situation, remembering all that had happened and deciding that he wasn't missing any limbs, though they were all a little on the toasty side, which meant he'd gotten frostbit.

Understandable, given that he'd been thrown buck-naked off a moving train into hip-deep snow on Christmas Eve! He ground his molars as he remembered Miss Mattie swinging that rock toward his head. He'd likely been brained good, scrambling his marbles, because his thinker box was a little on the fuzzy side. He couldn't decide if she'd been out to rob him or kill him because, learning who he was, she'd decided that she had reason to snuff his fuse.

Was she kin to someone he'd caused to swing from some federal gallows? Totally possible. God knew such indignant folks had tried to beef him before. That's why Longarm was usually pretty careful. He didn't take his clothes and gun off for just any girl. The last assignment in all that cold and snow up around the Canadian border must have really worn him out, caused him to throw common sense to the wind and let his guard down.

He couldn't for the life of him believe that the innocent Miss Mattie Johnson, schoolteacher from Minnesota on her way to her first job out Montana way, had tried to kill him and throw him, with help from some man he'd never seen but had sensed from the depths of semiconsciousness, off a moving train on Christmas Eve . . .

Longarm shook his head. You just couldn't tell about folks.

His heartbeat quickened when he remembered that he'd been ordered by Chief Marshal Billy Vail to Little Missouri City pronto, to see about some fiendish murderer on the loose and killing over thataway. Now Longarm would be late arriving at his next assignment, and how was he going to explain that to Billy?

"Sorry, Billy, but I got caught with my pants down and some frisky Frieda decided to brain me after I fucked her, before her pussy was even dry, and tossed me from the train."

Longarm shifted in the bed in frustration, and the bare-backed, chestnut-haired girl before him must have heard him or maybe seen his movement from the corner of her eye, because she suddenly lurched with a start and half turned toward him. Her breasts were extremely large, full, and firm, with big, dark areolas and thick nipples. They jounced together before, giving another gasp, she covered one with her sponge and the second with her other hand, though neither the sponge nor the hand could cover them completely.

The girl beetled her brows, which were a shade darker

than her chestnut hair. Her brown eyes flashed angrily. She grunted and snarled at him but otherwise said nothing coherent. At first Longarm thought she was reprimanding him for ogling her in some foreign tongue, but then he realized that she wasn't speaking any language at all but merely doing what she *seemed* to be doing—snarling and grunting and jutting her chin at him.

"I do apologize, miss!" Longarm said, throwing up his hands as though she were leveling a brace of pistols on him. "I didn't mean to snoop but I just woke up in this big comfortable bed, and . . . and . . . well, there you were . . . and, hell—you're so damn purty I thought I must surely be dreaming. That's why I didn't say anything!"

He grinned in an attempt to defuse her anger. Apparently, it worked.

She piped down. The anger leached from her eyes. She lowered her gaze, turned away from him, and, facing the washstand, pulled her dress back up over her breasts. She slid the straps up onto her shoulders. Sliding her hair back from her slightly flushed cheeks, she came over to stand beside the bed, gazing down at him critically.

She stared at him as though she weren't sure what to make of him, as though she were more than a little suspicious. He supposed that was understandable, since she'd found him buck-naked in the snow along the railroad tracks and all.

"I do appreciate the help, miss," Longarm said, meaning it. "You must have got to me just in time. Don't feel like I've lost any overly valuable parts." As he gazed up at her, he saw that she was staring at his lips.

Was she deaf as well as dumb? If so, she was the most
beautiful deaf-mute he'd ever laid eyes on. Full breasted,
round hipped, brown eyed, and chestnut haired. Her
face was heart shaped, with a pert nose and a wide,
frank mouth. As he reflected on the girl's beauty, he realized that he was naked under the quilts, blankets, and
sheets.

Not only naked but covered in something slippery.
The something must have been a salve of some kind.
Longarm also realized that his dick was at half-mast
beneath the covers. He was buried under so many quilts
and blankets that he didn't think it was noticeable, but
he squirmed around a little. She'd apparently already
seen him naked, but he was self-conscious about the
hard-on.

The girl leaned down and looked closely at his
cheeks. She touched a finger to the tip of his nose.
Checking for frostbite, he realized. Apparently satisfied
with how things looked on his head, she walked to the
foot of the bed and drew the quilts and blankets up from
the bottom, exposing his feet. She crouched to closely
inspect his toes, pinched the two big ones critically, then
straightened with a satisfied grunt and tucked the blankets back under the mattress.

Looking all business, pooching her ripe lips out
thoughtfully, she walked over beside him and lifted the
blankets there as well, exposing his groin, hips, and
belly. Longarm gritted his teeth.

"Uh . . . ah . . . excuse me there, miss, but . . ."

He felt the comparatively cool open air of the shack
waft in under the blankets and wrap around his dick,
which was still at half-mast. Even half-frozen, the damn

thing had a mind of its own. Staring up at his face, she reached under the covers and wrapped her hand around his cock.

"Oh," he said, feeling the appendage instantly grow harder. "Shit."

As she continued to stare up at him with those wide, lustrous brown eyes, she quirked her mouth corners knowingly, then slid her hand down from his cock to his balls. She prodded them with her fingers and then hefted both in her hands before wrapping her hand once more around his cock. She pumped him a couple of times, staring up at him, one eye crossing slightly as she grinned like the cat that ate the canary.

Longarm swallowed the knot in his throat as she manipulated him, causing his blood to rise. Suddenly, she removed her hand and shoved her head down under the covers. He felt her warm lips and moist mouth slide halfway down over his cock before they slid up and off him, and she pulled her head out from under the covers.

She smacked her lips, smiling devilishly at him, and tucked the covers back down around him. She tucked them down so snuggly that his hard-on was revealed, tenting the covers over his waist. She smiled at that, teasing him, and then Longarm saw a shadow pass outside the window to the right of the front door. Boots thumped on the stoop outside the place. The door opened, admitting a stocky, broad-shouldered gent wrapped in a long, thick bear coat and frost-rimed fur hat. The man's thick, salt-and-pepper mustache was also touched with frost, as were his eyebrows and lashes.

He held an armload of wood as he kicked the door

closed. The girl hadn't heard the man enter, but she must have felt the reverberation of the door slamming. She turned toward the man, who tossed the wood into the box beside a potbelly stove and said in a thick old-world accent, "Whoo-whee—it's a cold one out there this mornin', and that ain't no joke! Do believe my pecker froze to my leg. Might not be able to use the privy again till spring!"

As the stranger removed his hat, he lifted his big, chiseled red face with long, cobalt-blue eyes toward the low ceiling and laughed.

Chapter 7

"What about you there, friend?" the stranger said, walking toward Longarm. "You gonna be able to use the privy again in the spring?"

He chuckled and stood next to the girl, pulling the heavy deerskin mitten off his right hand and extending it to Longarm. The lawman could feel the cold air billowing off the gent. That's how cold it was outside. Remembering how he'd been tossed into all that snow and cold last night caused Longarm to give an involuntary shiver as he held out his own greasy hand to shake the stranger's.

"Custis Long," he said.

"Nikolai Akhmatova." The man's hand was as large as Longarm's, and strong. "This is Olga. I call her 'Perfect.' It better suits her."

"Perfect?" Longarm said. "How's that?"

"She is the perfect woman," Akhmatova said,

wrapping an arm around the girl's shoulders. "She is both deaf and dumb, but she works like a Missouri mule!"

Akhmatova, whom Longarm judged to be around fifty, possibly sixty, threw his head back again, roaring so loudly that the sunlit, frosted windows tinkled in their frames. Olga snarled and gave him a hard elbow to the ribs, apparently understanding the old sport's humor and not approving. She swung away from Longarm and strode into the kitchen part of the small cabin, where a range ticked and several pots bubbled.

The old man winced and rubbed the rib she'd bruised, then continued chuckling as he said, "Takes after her mother, she does—God rest the poor woman's soul."

He looked at Longarm askance, slit-eyed, suddenly wary. "And just who threw you from the train last night, Mr. Long?"

"Deputy U.S. Marshal Long," Longarm said, rubbing the tender spot on his temple where Mattie had brained him. "That's one hell of a long story, and one I'm not overly proud of, I'm afraid. If it's all the same to you, I'd just as soon not go into overmuch detail."

"Ah, you're a lawman." The old man continued to seem skeptical.

"There should be a badge in my wallet." It dawned on Longarm that his clothes were likely still aboard the train. "Oh, Lordy," he said. He supposed his guns were still on the train as well.

The old man must have read his mind. He hooked a long red thumb toward a wooden bench running along the front wall of the cabin, between the left wall and the door. Longarm saw his clothes neatly folded on the bench, his frock coat and buckskin mackinaw hanging from hooks in the wall. What appeared to be his saddle was on the bench itself, his gun belt and holstered Colt .44 coiled beside it. A rifle he assumed was his, for it was a Winchester '73, leaned against the wall near the saddle and the pistol.

"Not to worry—whoever threw you from the train, Marshal Long, must not have wanted any nasty reminders of your presence." Akhmatova chuckled as he shrugged out of his heavy bear coat and hung it on a peg near Longarm's mackinaw. "There was no wallet, though. At least, me and Olga didn't find one."

Longarm was both grateful and flabbergasted they'd found what they had. "You found all that stuff in the *snow?*"

The old man sat on the bench to kick out of his heavy boots, which were sewn from deer hide and rabbit skins. "We were driving back from a Christmas dance at the church last night when we stopped to let the train pass. Just as we did, you came flying off that train and into the snow. *Puff!* Never seen a man roll so long and kick up so much snow!"

The Russian slapped his knee and laughed until his eyes watered.

"And then, as the train continued on, moving sort of slow because it was climbing a hill, all that stuff over there came flying out after you. I would have missed your rifle but I stepped on it and it nearly caused me to slip and fall! Sorry I couldn't find your wallet."

"That's all right. I got a feelin' my wallet prob'ly never made it off the train."

"You think you was robbed?"

"Somethin' like that." Unless Mattie had harbored a special grudge against Longarm, there was little explanation for her motivation aside from robbery. She was probably traveling with a man. That was usually how such confidence schemes worked.

"What's the world comin' to, huh—when even lawmen ain't safe ridin' the train!"

"Mr. Akhmatova, Miss Olga," Longarm said, shaking his head slowly in awe at his undeserved good fortune. If he'd lost only his wallet, a few dollars, and his badge, he was damn lucky. "I don't know how to thank you two. I really don't." He sat up and slipped a leg over the side of the bed. "But if you'll both be kind enough to turn away, I reckon I'd best get dressed. I got urgent business in Little Missouri Cit . . ."

He let his voice trail off as the room slid up sharply on the left and then slowly leveled out but only to slide up again on the right. He sagged back on the bed, bringing a hand to his temple. Fatigue weighed on him, heavy as a blacksmith's anvil.

"Whoa," he said.

Akhmatova laughed. "I don't think so, Marshal Long. That's quite a knot you got on your noggin there. And she was quite a tumble you took from the train. I don't think you're going anywhere. Not till tomorrow, anyways. Besides, it's Christmas! You must stay and help us celebrate! We are all alone here on our humble farm, and only eight miles from Little Missouri City. Tomorrow, if you are well enough, I, Nikolai, will drive you to town in the wagon. Unless we get another big snowfall, of course. Then you may not be going anywhere until spring!"

The broad-shouldered Russian slapped his thigh again and roared at the ceiling.

Meanwhile, as Longarm lifted his leg onto the bed and lay back against the scrolled wooden headboard, Olga carried toward him a tray bearing a steaming soup tureen, a thick wedge of crusty, brown, thickly buttered bread, and a glass of thick, creamy milk. Longarm had been smelling several different succulent aromas since he'd first awakened, but his stomach couldn't seem to make up its mind whether it was hungry enough for the assault of food on it.

But now, as the girl set the tray down on the small table beside the bed and he got a look at the wedge of buttery bread and the brown soup in which several chunks of what appeared to be venison, carrots, and onions floated in fat-cloudy broth, his stomach growled and his mouth watered.

He thought he might be able to take a sip and a bite or two.

He was right. When the girl started feeding him and the rich, fatty, hearty soup hit his stomach, he grew hungrier and hungrier. Enough of his strength returned that after she'd fed him half the bowl of soup he was able to take over the spooning himself. While she returned to the kitchen to feed Nikolai—her father, apparently—and to tend her pots and pans, Longarm polished off the soup and swabbed the bowl of the final delicious vestiges with his last scrap of bread. He packed it all down with the rest of the milk, probably fresh that very morning.

Olga had no sooner taken the tray away than Longarm's eyelids grew heavy and he felt his head and his well-padded belly sagging back into the bed. He slept the deepest sleep of his life.

When he awoke, it took him nearly a full minute to remember where he was. The cabin's windows had turned from being brightly lit to cobalt blue. It was late afternoon or early evening. The little candles bedecking the Christmas tree had been lit. They smoked and fluttered in the drafts that scurried around the little sod shanty like invisible rats.

Olga stood a few feet off the foot of the bed, filling a square, corrugated tin washtub with steaming water from a copper boiler. She looked over at Longarm and smiled, then returned to the stove, from which she retrieved another steaming kettle, and poured the water into the tub, giving him another oblique smile through the rising steam.

Longarm looked around. Her father, Nikolai, was nowhere to be seen. His heavy fur coat was gone from the hook on the wall.

When Olga had added some cool water to the steaming tub, she dragged a chair out from the table, positioning it near the tub, and set a thick towel and a cake of soap on it. Then she turned toward Longarm, smiled that strange little smile of hers, as though she knew a nasty secret from deep in his past, and then slid her dress down her arms.

It tumbled to her waist, leaving her heavy breasts bare. She continued smiling at him in that shrewd way and then pushed the dress down over her full hips and well-turned thighs until it lay in a pile at her slender feet.

The bush between her thighs was dark and tangled.

Naked, her heavy breasts jostling, she walked over to the table and used a few pins to secure her long hair in a prettily messy bun atop her head. Then she walked over to the tub and tested the temperature with a toe. She gave a satisfied grunt, stepped into the water, and, placing her hands on the sides of the tub, slowly lowered herself to her knees, her breasts sloping out from her chest.

She looked up at Longarm again and bit her lower lip. He was fully erect under the heavy covers, which was obvious by the hump in the star quilt, and he no longer cared if she knew it.

Of course, getting him hard had been the nasty little succubus's full intention, though why she felt compelled to torture him so, he had no idea. He supposed a pretty deaf-mute could feel especially isolated, living way out here with just her old man in the frozen wilds of Dakota Territory. Maybe she'd never been fucked before, though something told Longarm that wasn't so. It was no truer for Olga than it had been for Mattie.

Like Mattie, this girl had had plenty of practice performing her special kind of frisky feminine witchery.

There was little to nothing Longarm could do about the torture he was suffering except watch her, fascinated, and hope she decided to finish the maneuver she'd given him a sample of before her old man had walked into the shanty.

She lowered her face to the water in the small tub and, using the soap and a cloth, washed it thoroughly. She scrubbed the back of her neck and behind her ears and then she went to work on her neck before resoaping the cloth, working up some heavy suds, and slowly massaging each heavy breast in turn. While she did so, she kept her smoky gaze on Longarm, looking down only occasionally at her slick, jostling breasts, making sure she covered every inch.

Satisfied she'd cleaned her chest and belly, she stood up in the tub and soaped and scrubbed her legs and feet, sliding the cloth between her toes. She squatted without show of any modesty whatever to clean her pussy and the crack between her butt cheeks, grunting and groaning as she worked. And then she sat down in the tub and splashed the water over her entire body, rinsing off the suds. Her last chore was to hook her arms over her shoulders and saw the stretched, soapy cloth across her back.

Longarm enjoyed the show as she twisted and turned in the confining tub, her face attractively strained and flushed from the effort.

She rinsed again and then got out and toweled herself off, giving Longarm another show. And then, still naked, she walked over to the bed and pulled the covers back, revealing Longarm's long, thick, muscular body and fully erect dong, which angled back over his belly button, jerking with each heavy, thudding beat of his heart.

He was hoping she would climb on top of him and fuck him, but instead she gently helped him to a standing position and then walked him over to the tub, grunting and groaning out incoherent orders as she did. It wasn't hard to understand, however, that it was his turn to take a bath—in the same water she'd bathed in. For some reason, the notion caused especially sharp pangs of lust to shoot up the backs of his legs to prod his scrotum, causing his cock to grow so hard it felt ready to burst like an overcooked sausage.

Of course, it didn't help that her big tits were jouncing against his arm.

Olga grunted and pointed at the soapy water, and after Longarm had dropped to his butt inside the tub, where the water was still warm but not hot, the girl walked over to the potbelly stove. She stuffed several chunks of split oak and pine through the door, gave it a stir with another chunk, and then tossed that chunk as well into the conflagration.

The fire roared. The stove ticked and crackled. The shanty grew instantly warmer, fogging the frosted windows that were growing ever darker. In fact, only some periwinkle blue remained in the sky over the pale expanse of snow rolling away beyond the front windows.

Longarm wondered where old Nikolai was. He also wondered what would happen if the stocky Russian returned to find Longarm and his daughter naked together. The girl didn't seem overly worried about it, so Longarm decided not to worry about it, either.

He grabbed the cloth and the soap, but just then Olga squatted down beside the tub, grabbed the soap and cloth away from him with a grunt, and began scrubbing his back. As she did, her breasts jostled like water flasks hanging from a saddle horn. Longarm couldn't help but grab one, heft it in his hand, and roll the nipple jutting from the large areola between his thumb and index finger.

Olga groaned loudly as he manipulated her tits, but she continued to work industriously at scrubbing his broad chest and shoulders and his thick, corded arms. She reached between his legs to scrub his erection and his balls, throwing more wood, so to speak, on his own inner fire. While she did, he shuttled his gaze between her face and her hands that worked so adroitly and practically over him.

Olga set the rag and the soap aside and then dumped cool water over his head, rinsing him. Longarm grunted at the sudden contrast in water temperature and felt his cock instantly begin to soften.

"Good Lord, girl," Longarm castigated her, blowing the tepid water out from between his lips. "What're you tryin' to do—kill me?"

She grunted and gestured for him to stand.

He stood. He figured she'd hand him a towel but instead she remained on her knees. She stared up at his cock, which was hanging at half-mast. She leaned her head over the tub, stuck out her tongue, and touched the tip of it to the tip of his cock. The thick snake bobbed its head and instantly started to rise to attention.

Longarm groaned.

Olga moaned and grunted as she sucked the swollen head of his cock for a time. Then, when he was back even harder than before, his blood fairly boiling, she wrapped her hand around his shaft and gently began to pump him. She opened a tin of salve and worked the salve into the palms of both her hands, and then she massaged it into his cock and balls. She worked very slowly, massaging his balls with one hand, very slowly sliding her hand up and down his raging hard-on with her other hand, drawing the foreskin up and over the swollen mushroom head and back down again.

The salve snapped and crackled in her hands.

While Olga continued with the expert hand job, she smiled up at Longarm from beneath her brows. Her breasts rose and fell heavily as she breathed through her half-open mouth, occasionally running her pink tongue across her full upper lip.

Longarm rocked back on his heels in the tub, clenching his fists and grinding his teeth. His blood was rising, rising, rising.

She pumped him harder and faster. She continued increasing the pace of her pumping until she was gritting her teeth and grunting and pumping wildly with both hands.

Longarm cursed.

His come jettisoned from his cock to baste her cheeks.

What didn't hit Olga careened nearly four feet beyond the tub to sizzle against the stove.

Longarm returned to bed, sated and exhausted and certain that, out here in Dakota on Christmas Day, he'd received the best hand job of his life.

Chapter 8

The Reverend waved his hand at the hot, smelly steam gushing from the big locomotive's pressure relief valves and said, "Pee-u. That stinks worse than a possum's fart!"

Mattie poked her fingers in her ears against the clattering and thundering and general caterwauling of the train that was just then sliding away behind her along the tracks, continuing west. She turned to look at the Pullman car in which she'd fucked the lawman and had received only twenty-four dollars for her efforts—you'd think a federal badge-toter would make more than that for risking life and limb every day of his dangerous career for the good citizens of this country!—and felt her mouth corners draw down as though from a sudden hard pull of gravity.

The train cars continued to gain speed as they slid off down the tracks. Then the little red caboose slid past, and the conductor, bundled in a heavy wool coat and muffler, waved a green wooden paddle out to the side, giving the engineer in the locomotive the all-clear signal.

The conductor stopped waving the paddle and turned to glance back toward Mattie and the Reverend, who were the only two passengers standing on the snowy wooden platform on the west end of the plank board shack that served as the depot building of Little Missouri City, Dakota Territory. He offered a wan, sympathetic smile to the pair, touched two gloved fingers to the leather bill of his watch cap in grim farewell, and then turned to enter the caboose, quickly closing the door on the subzero cold.

Thinking of the fire that the conductor probably had burning in that cozy little car, Mattie gave a shiver against the cold pressing against her like a giant's invisible hand. She stared off down the tracks, the caboose and its door growing smaller and smaller, the gray smoke curling from the tin chimney pipe poking out of the caboose's roof growing fainter and fainter, until the little car dropped down into a swale and was gone with the rest of the train.

She turned to stare south along what she presumed to be the main street of this nowhere little town all but buried in snow. The sun reflected so brightly off the snow that Mattie had to shield her eyes against it. When they finally somewhat adjusted to the glare, she saw that there couldn't have been more than ten frame or mud-brick business buildings lining the wide main street, which wasn't more than two city blocks long. Around the business district in all directions, including behind the railroad tracks and depot hut, lay the rest of the town. The sod or log shanties, barns, stock pens, privies, and hitch-and-rail or unpeeled log corrals looked so gray and worn-out and forlorn, hunched there in the knee-deep snow, that Mattie found herself starting to sob.

"Don't you dare!" the Reverend said, repeating, "Don't you dare cry, you little harlot! You got us into this fix, now you just dry those eyes and try to help me think of a way out of it."

"I didn't get us into nothin'!" Mattie screeched, wheeling toward the tall, thin gent from Tennessee and her partner in confidence schemes. "We didn't have to get off here in the middle of nowhere! That was your crazy idea!"

"It was my idea to save our sorry asses because you couldn't leave well enough alone of that federal lawman's donkey dong!"

The Reverend must have sensed that someone was inhabiting the little shack, for he glanced to his left at the building, from which gray smoke rose from a tin chimney pipe, and then turned back to Mattie, lowering his voice considerably.

"Sooner or later," he ground out through gritted teeth, "the porter or someone else was going to realize the marshal was missing. And when that happened, they'd ask around to see if anyone had seen him. Of course, everyone in the car in which you'd met him had seen you two retire together, and they'd report as much to the porter. Which would make you—and thus *me*—look suspicious as hell!"

"You're being overly dramatic again, Reverend," Mattie said, loosing another sob as she turned to look at the motley little town—if you could even call it a town. It was a little more substantial than the Denver stockyards but appeared a whole lot less occupied by men as well as beasts, though the former were most likely huddled by fires in their chilly lairs. "Oh, how did we get stuck up here so late in the year?"

Having worked a few towns in the upper Midwest over the summer, they'd intended to be in Seattle by now and be working their way down the Pacific Coast.

"I reckon we simply misjudged the shortness of the Yankee summer," the Reverend said, drawing out that last in his way so it sounded like "soomahh." "Don't worry, my dear," he added, slinging the long leather lanyards of his two large carpetbags over his shoulders, "we won't tarry here long. Another train will no doubt be through next week. If we play our cards right—proverbially speaking, of course—we might even leave with a little extra cash so that we can travel in style the rest of the way to Seattle and then down to Portland." He stepped down off the snowy, frosty planking of the platform and into the snowy street, limping on his bad ankle. "Come along, dear. Surely someone around here can stir us up a couple of toddies . . ."

Mattie hefted her leather accordion bag and one large carpetbag with a groan, and began following the Reverend along the middle of the street. A good foot of recently fallen snow lay in the street, unmarked saved for what appeared to be a single wagon and maybe two horseback riders, and it feathered up over her shins as she walked.

She was wearing underwear this morning—heavy woolen socks and pantaloons beneath her thick velvet winter dress that hugged her tightly at the waist and was considerably higher cut than the one she had worn on the train and which she used to trap fools such as the marshal. She would have snickered at the memory of the night before, but, unfortunately, the joke seemed to now be on her.

Despite her heavy clothes, the snow still chilled her legs. In fact, her cheeks and nose were already numb, and her toes ached desperately despite the fur lining of her side-button leather shoes.

The Reverend stopped and turned to his left to regard an unsound, two-story, wood-frame building with faded and badly chipped light blue paint. The broad sign over the front verandah announced THE BLUE DOG SALOON. What most impressed the Reverend as well as young Mattie was the gray smoke billowing thickly from two stovepipes jutting from the shack's gently pitched, shake-shingled roof.

The Reverend looked around and said with a defeated air, "Well, this looks like about the only place in town we might find shelter, so I reckon the Blue Dog it is."

Lugging her bags, Mattie followed the Reverend up the steps, which had been swept of snow, and through the heavy winter door. She awkwardly kicked the door shut behind her and then turned to the room, blinking to help her eyes adjust to the thick gloom as the smells of stale tobacco, spilled beer, wet wool, and unwashed men assaulted her not overly delicate senses.

Three men who were gathered at a table about two-thirds of the way down the room, beyond a Christmas tree and ticking wood-burning stove, turned quick, scrutinizing looks on the two newcomers. A large man with a soft, womanish face stood behind the bar on the room's left side, but it was the stove that Mattie was most interested in. She felt pushed toward it by an unseen hand. She felt downright proprietary about the heat, having gotten such a brazen taste of how rare it likely was in these parts, and how quickly the cold could leach your life away and leave you a lifeless lump in the Dakota snow.

She was glad no one was sitting near it. She walked toward it, set down her bags with a relieved sigh, turned a chair toward the stove, and slacked into the seat. She closed her eyes, enjoying the push of the dry heat against her face, instantly chasing the brittle chill from her blood and bones.

"Oh," she heard herself say.

Meanwhile, the Reverend scrutinized the room from behind his square, red-lensed, spectacles—after he'd rubbed the frost from them, that is—and then sauntered in his dandyish way, grinning his minister's smile at the big, lumpy gent standing behind the bar in bib-front overalls and a red flannel shirt. Opening her eyes as well as her coat, Mattie watched the Tennessean set his bags down on the floor and say to the gent behind the bar, "Nice, warm place you have here, Mister, uh . . ."

"Jenny," the person said, and instantly Mattie saw that the womanish man or mannish woman was indeed the latter. Her voice was deep but distinctly feminine. She did not shake the Reverend's proffered hand but glanced quickly—nervously?—between the three men sitting at the table near the stairs, and Mattie.

Mattie saw that all three men had their eyes on her, and she instantly drew her chin down and folded her arms across her breasts, wanting in no way to encourage any of the three to make a play for her.

She was in no mood for schemes, and that's all that would have interested her about such a rough-looking trio, anyway. Even on the warmest of days and in the best of circumstances, she was not in the market for companionship. She wished the Reverend would hurry back and reinforce the notion that they were together, even though she was supposed to be "the preacher's" sister. All she wanted was food and warmth and a good bed to curl up in until the next train came through.

Merry fucking Christmas, she thought, glancing at the pathetic-looking pine tree sporting a few measly strings of drab-looking tinsel.

At the bar, the Reverend lowered his hand, which the mannish Miss Jenny did not shake, and said, "I do apologize for the mistake, my good woman. My glasses are still a little frosty. Cold outside, you know. Say, as we're just off the train—my sister and I, the Reverend and Mattie Teakettle—we were wondering if you have anything with which to mix us a couple of toddies."

"Why on earth did you get off the train here of all places, Reverend?" Jenny asked, studying the man with the slow-as-blackstrap Southern accent critically and then once more shuttling her gaze between the three cold-blooded killers and the Reverend's sister sitting hunched by the stove. "Do you know just where in hell you are?"

Yes, hell was correct, the owner of the Blue Dog silently reflected. Especially now with those three still here, abusing Miss Evangeline up in her room every few hours and generally keeping the town under siege. Apparently, they were waiting for the rest of their gang, who was very slow to turn up. Probably due to the cold, Jenny thought, though she didn't know if she wanted the others to get here or not. Only if it meant that they would *all* leave then.

These three were causing enough trouble as it was.

Turns out, Little Missouri City didn't have one real man in it. If it did, he would have snuck into the Blue Dog and shot these miscreants while they'd slept, though they admittedly slept intermittently, rarely all at the same time, and at odd hours.

"Yes, the town is Little Missouri City, is it not?" the almost grotesquely thin, cobalt-eyed gent with the syrupy accent said, smiling behind his weird glasses. One silver eyetooth glinted in the bright sunlight pushing through the front windows. "Not a mile out of town, the voice of the Lord told me that my sister and I must detrain here . . . and bring His word to this snow-locked little town." He winked behind the glasses and smiled disarmingly, so that Jenny had to admit the gent had a certain oddly comforting charm.

"You're . . . uh . . . bringin' us the Word, Reverend?" Jenny asked.

"Well, I'd like to. It is Christmas, after all. First, however, the toddies?" The disarming, damn near enchanting smile appeared again.

"Toddies," Jenny said, looking around. "Yeah, all right—I can mix you a coupla toddies. How's bourbon and hot water and a coupla pinches of brown sugar?"

The Southern preacher rubbed his palms together.

"Sounds downright heavenly, my good lady! Downright heavenly!"

"All right," Jenny said. "I got some hot water on the range for tea. I'll fetch it."

She pushed through the curtained doorway, fetched the iron pot of steaming water, and pushed back through the curtain. She built two toddies, adding a pinch of brown sugar to each. As she did, the preacher, his eager eyes on the steaming drinks, said, "I was wondering if it might be possible, it being Christmas and all, if my dear sister and I could hold a little Christmas service . . . right here in your saloon, Miss Jenny. It bein' Christmas and all!"

"And then, after the service, the good Reverend Teakettle and his buxom li'l sis could pass a hat for money to give to the three-toed, humpbacked orphans over in Reno or Salt Lake or maybe Seattle." This from Emory Drake, who, much to Jenny's chagrin, had silently climbed up out of his chair and strode slowly, menacingly, over to where the preacher stood on the other side of the bar from Jenny.

Curly Jenkins and Vincent McKirk were grinning over at him, their eyes shiny from drink. They'd managed to stay drunk for the past three days, ever since they'd first pulled into Little Missouri City.

"Uh . . . that would be the *blind* orphans in *Cheyenne*, my good man," the Reverend said, turning to the short, thick, evil bastard just now resting an elbow on the bar about six feet away from him. "Orphaned and blinded due to no fault of their own . . ."

Drake smiled knowingly at him.

That appeared to make the man of the cloth nervous.

He frowned and extended his long, pale, beringed hand to the outlaw, saying, "I'm Reverend Teakettle. And you're . . ."

"Drake," the outlaw said, ignoring the taller man's proffered hand.

"And you ain't no Reverend Teakettle," Drake added, swelling his nostrils. "You're Horace Clancy. We rode together in the Twenty-Fourth Regiment, Tennessee Regulars. You was *Lieutenant* Horace Clancy at the time, your pappy havin' bought you a commission so's you wouldn't have to mix with all us unwashed Rebs and tote one o' them heavy Springfield rifles, lug a rucksack, and dodge Union minie balls."

Suddenly angry, Vincent McKirk jerked his chair back loudly and stood, glaring at the Reverend—or whoever in hell he was. "Yeah, I remember 'String Bean' Lieutenant Clancy," he said, gaunt cheeks paling with anger. "When things got ugly at Chickamauga, he shot himself in the ankle and spent the rest of the war back at his pappy's cotton plantation, healin' up in a big feather bed while the rest of us Regulars fought and died bloody—so beat-up and shot and blown to hell that all we could do was *watch Atlanta burn!*"

"Oh, no—oh, dear!" a voice screamed in Jenny's ears. "Oh, no—oh, *dear!*"

Chapter 9

"That will be enough!" intoned the pretty blonde, standing now and glaring at the outlaws. "This man, Reverend Teakettle, is my brother. I would certainly know my brother, would I not, and I promise you he is not . . . *certainly not this* . . . this . . . Lieutenant *Horace Whoever-You-Said-He-Was!* The Reverend and I, his sister, are in the service of the disenfranchised members of our pitiless society, and that is what has found us out so far from home on this cold Christmas Day in Dakota Territory."

She shifted her wary, indignant eyes around the outlaws, who appeared to be having none of it.

"I assure you!" she insisted, stomping a heel down loudly.

The Reverend picked up his and the girl's steaming toddies. "I assure you, dear fellow," he said amiably as he began moving toward the girl, his gaze on Drake, "you simply have me confused with another Southerner."

"I do, do I?"

The Reverend had taken four limping steps, and then he stopped and looked down at his left ankle as though he'd only just then noticed it was bowed out on the inside. It looked as though he had a goiter, though on his leg rather than his neck. Jenny had thought his affliction was something similar when he'd first limped into the saloon with the girl. Now the saloon owner's pulse quickened, and she raked her gaze across the three outlaws, Drake and McKirk glaring down at the Reverend's gimpy foot—or was he indeed the former Lieutenant Clancy?—while Curly Jenkins grinned diabolically at the girl, whose face had gone as red as a summer sunset.

Jenkins lifted an arm and thrust a pointing finger out at the girl, intoning, "And that there is Arlis Watson. I seen her perform in Leadville a few years back. Shit, even at thirteen or fourteen years old, she was all filled out. Man, could she make her titties dance while she pranced across them stages in nothin' more than high-heeled shoes and feathers in her hair!"

He clapped his hands and lifted a guffaw to the ceiling. "Hello, there, Arlis! Remember me—ole redheaded Curly Jenkins? What's the matter—you get tired of wriggling your ass and shakin' your tits, and take up with this cowardly, gutter-suckin' son of a bitch to run confidence schemes? On *Christmas Day?* In *Dakota-fuckin'-Territory?*" He laughed again, louder. "Oh, that's *rich!*"

Drake suddenly moved on the Reverend. The stocky

outlaw reached forward to pull the Reverend's coat open. There was a loud *crash* as the two toddies hit the floor simultaneously, the clay mugs shattering and the hot liquid spreading across the floorboards. Drake screamed and jerked back, clamping his left hand to his right side.

For a moment, the entire room fell silent, all five figures in the room before Jenny suddenly turning to stone. The world hiccupped and time stopped for two or three brief seconds. All eyes, including Jenny's, were on Drake. The thick outlaw pulled his hand away from his side. Crimson blood smeared the fingers that he raised slowly to his face.

"Bastard *cut* me!" the outlaw bellowed, jerking his eyes toward the knife that Jenny just then saw clutched in the Reverend's left fist. The tip of the knife, too, was coated in red.

"Make another move like that, Drake," the Reverend shouted hoarsely, showing his teeth under his dark brown mustache, "and I'll gut you like a fish, string your little balls, and hang 'em around my neck!"

Vincent McKirk's right hand jerked toward a pistol on his right hip. The Reverend became a blur of quick motion. The blade of his knife flashed in the bright light pushing through the saloon's frosty windows. There was a brief whirling sound followed by a dull, crunching *thud*.

Vincent McKirk grunted and stepped back, his right hand fluttering around the grips of the pistol he had not yet managed to lift from its holster. His other hand rose heavily toward his chest, the fingers brushing the walnut handle of the knife protruding from his breastbone. The

knife was buried hilt-deep. Blood oozed out around the
blade to stain the man's pin-striped, cream-colored shirt
over which he wore a shabby wool vest.

"Oh, dear God!" Jenny heard herself scream beneath
another shrill, inarticulate scream that she only later
realized had been loosed by the girl—the Reverend's
sister, or Miss Arlis Watson, or whoever-in-hell-
she-was.

Because a second after that, everything got really,
briefly crazy as, flinching, she watched the Reverend
pull a small, silver-plated revolver from somewhere
on his person and take aim at Emory Drake. Only,
Drake had two of his own pistols out by then. Both of
Drake's revolvers roared, then roared again, stabbing
smoke and flames at the former Lieutenant Clancy and
sending him into a bizarre death dance toward the front
door.

Clancy fired his little pocket pistol into the floor near
his prancing boots, bounced off one of the front windows, and dropped to the floor on his butt. His red-
lensed glasses dangled from one ear as he slowly sagged
sideways before coming to rest on his left shoulder, quivering as his life left him.

When Clancy was dead and Drake and Jenkins saw
that their partner McKirk was also dead, Drake simply
ordered another drink and some bandages as he sagged
into a chair, clutching his cut right side, and Curly Jenkins hauled the girl kicking and screaming up the stairs
at the back of the room.

Jenny fetched Drake a new bottle and some strips
of cotton bandage, sobbing and wishing like hell the

town constable, Emmitt Grassley, would get off his sorry, cowardly ass and *do* something.

Not long after Longarm had received the best hand job of his life and had taken a short but restful nap while Olga puttered about the kitchen cooking Christmas supper, Nikolai returned to the Akhmatova cabin on an icy draft of wintery air.

The old Russian, his mustache and brows white with frost, had been off cutting wood along a river bottom. He'd shot a deer along the river bottom as well, to be used for the traditional Akhmatova Christmas stew, and as soon as he dropped the frozen, bloody burlap pouch containing a stout venison roast onto Olga's cutting table, the girl got right to work preparing the stew.

Soon, the cabin was filled with succulent, soothing smells of deer meat stewing with onions and potatoes, complemented wonderfully by the fragrance of baking bread and the fruity aroma of plum pudding. When Nikolai had washed and donned a red-and-gold quilted smock and a pair of wool-lined deerskin moccasins for the occasion, the old Russian poured himself and Longarm each a full mug of the chokecherry wine he brewed himself. Longarm tried to get up and sit in a chair, but both Nikolai and his doting daughter insisted he stay in bed and continue to rest.

"You can enjoy Christmas as well there as in a chair," Nikolai boomed out, filling Longarm's fist with a mug of the dark red wine. "Besides, as my wine has an extra kick for the vodka I add when I bottle it, you won't have so far to stagger when you pass out!"

The old man guffawed and stomped his boot at that, and then he sagged into a rocker and, conversing idly with Longarm while Olga cooked, he took up his fiddle and tuned it.

The meal tasted as wonderful as it smelled, although Longarm felt a little ridiculous being served in bed as though he were an invalid. After supper, when Olga had cleared the table and Longarm and Nikolai had each enjoyed another mug of vodka-spiced wine, Nikolai played the fiddle while Olga danced tirelessly for nearly two straight hours. She danced traditional Russian Christmas dances, spinning and jouncing, hair flying, snapping her fingers and clapping her hands while Longarm clapped as well, and Nikolai stomped a boot while he played in his rocking chair, keeping time.

The pair did not bank the fire in the stove, douse the lamps and candles, and drift off to bed in the loft until long after midnight.

Longarm, drunk from the wine and horny from watching the girl dance, had trouble pissing into the thunder mug that was stowed beneath the bed. Finally, he collapsed and fell instantly asleep until he was roused by a brusque hand jerking his shoulder.

He opened his eyes with a start to see the unmistakable silhouette of Olga lift a gauzy nightgown up over her head and then toss it onto the floor. By the moonlight pushing through the frosty windows, Longarm watched the naked girl pull his covers back. She grunted, breathless, as she crawled up onto the bed, bent down, her hair deliciously raking his thighs and belly, and licked his cock until it was fully engorged.

She straddled him, rubbed her snatch with the head

of his shaft until she was wet enough for an easy union. And then, with a long, contented sigh, squeezing her eyes closed, she dropped slowly down his length until she was sitting on his hips. Her pussy contracted and expanded around him.

Olga rose up the length of his shaft once more, sucking air through her teeth, and then commenced fucking him—slowly at first but with a definite purposefulness. She continued to gather speed until she was a runaway horse heading for the barn, bouncing up and down, hair flying, causing the leather springs to squawk and the headboard to hammer the wall.

Longarm gritted his teeth, sure that old Nikolai would hear the torrid coupling and come running down from the loft with a loaded shotgun. But nothing like that happened. Olga came within six or seven minutes, and her spasming caused Longarm to come as well. Afterward, she cleaned them both with an old rag, kissed the lawman's nose and then, chuckling, his cock, and retreated back up the stairs to the loft.

Longarm shook his head, sighed, rested his head back against his pillow, and slept.

He woke the next morning feeling refreshed. His head no longer hurt and the burning numbness from the frostbite seemed to have been worked out of his body by Olga's salve.

Or had it been her ferocious lovemaking that had pushed the blood back into his extremities and obliterated the pain in his head?

Whatever the cause, he was glad to be feeling fit as a fiddle. He needed to get over to Little Missouri City and see about the dead lawmen. He'd been a fool to get

suckered into Mattie's scheme on the train, and to lose
a day getting to town. But, damnit, he'd just finished a
job. Who could blame him for wanting to let his hair
down a little? Especially when it was Christmas and so
cold even the devil himself, ole Scratch, likely had ici-
cles hanging from his horns.

Chief Marshal Vail—that's who could blame him. If
Billy ever found out about his senior deputy's fuckup,
that is. That didn't seem likely, as Longarm wasn't in
the habit of confessing all of his sundry sins and indis-
cretions in his work reports. If he had been, he'd likely
have gotten fired a long time ago and would now be
breaking rock in the Comstock Lode.

Longarm dressed and enjoyed an early, hearty breakfast with Olga and old Nikolai. He thanked the man for
his offer to drive Longarm into town in a buckboard
wagon, but said he'd prefer a saddle horse stout enough
to carry him through the deep snow between the
Akhmatova farm and Little Missouri City. Nikolai
winked and nodded and went out to saddle and lead a
beefy Percheron back to the cabin.

The shaggy beast looked nearly as large as a buffalo,
standing out there in the snowy yard, the sun glistening
off its cinnamon coat, jets of steam pluming from its
nostrils. Longarm gathered up his gear but before Nikolai would let him go, he made his guest throw back a
shot of vodka.

"Keep you warm on the way to town," said the old
Russian, throwing back a shot of his own. He looked
warily out the window. "Besides, I think a storm is brewing. No clouds yet, but I feel it in my bones. Yes, Marshal

Long, I think you will need that vodka in you for the trip to town. It might just get colder yet!"

Olga wrapped a heavy red muffler around Longarm's neck and knotted it tightly. She frowned and grunted, communicating in her own inarticulate way, and then glanced quickly, furtively at her father. When Nikolai had looked away with a wry snort, Olga planted a quick kiss on Longarm's nose.

Flushed with embarrassment, she hurried into the kitchen and busied herself with cleaning the breakfast dishes.

Longarm glanced at Nikolai, who gave him a knowing wink.

Feeling his own cheeks warm, Longarm pinched his hat brim to the man, went outside, mounted the big Percheron, and rode out through the farm's gate to the main road that would take him to town.

Chapter 10

An hour later, Longarm reined up on a hill overlooking Little Missouri City, which lay half-buried under a thick blanket of heavy snow.

Old Nikolai had been right about the weather changing. Clouds had moved in, sealing off the sky. Pelletlike flakes were now tumbling out of low gray clouds to be whipped this way and that in a brittle breeze. The pale light painted the snow on the ground a murky gray-blue. In contrast, the log and mud-brick buildings of the town nestled in a shallow bowl on the other side of the hill looked especially bleak and dark, poking up like ruins from the blue snow.

The train station lay down the hill to Longarm's right. He'd paralleled the all-but-buried tracks for the past two miles and could see them stretching away from the shabby little depot station at the north end of the town. The twin rails were ushered along by a single strand of telegraph wire strung between spindly poles. Except the wire had been cut, both cut ends drooping to the ground on the near end of the depot station.

The sight of those cut wires tightened the muscles between Longarm's shoulder blades. He reached forward on his right to pull his Winchester from its saddleboot. Removing the deerskin mitten from over the glove he wore on his right hand, he cocked the weapon one-handed, then lowered the hammer to half cock and returned the rifle to its scabbard.

He tightened the red muffler Olga had given him. The scarf was wrapped over his head, snug beneath his hat, and knotted beneath his chin. He was grateful for the girl's post-Christmas gift.

The muffler had likely kept his ears from freezing off.

He stuffed his right-hand mitten into a pocket of his buckskin mackinaw. A mitten prevented a man from triggering a gun. Instantly, he felt the cold penetrating his leather glove, but he'd have to endure the discomfort. Trouble had obviously come to Little Missouri City, as evidenced by the cut telegraph wire. He had no idea if it remained in the town or had moved on.

Only one way to find out.

The ends of his knotted scarf fluttering in the breeze beneath his chin, Longarm touched boot heals to the Percheron's flanks. The horse moved off down the hill, hooves crunching the snow. He and the stout horse crossed a shallow creek and then made a wide left swing to enter the town between the depot station on the right and a large, boarded-up mercantile on the left. A small barbershop, its windows shuttered, sat beside the mercantile, dwarfed by the much larger but apparently abandoned building.

The wind moaned softly. Fresh flakes a little larger than lice fluttered down from the cold gray sky, scratching along the surface of the snow that lay with a thin, crusted surface upon the broad main street of the town. Each of the Percheron's hooves punched easily through it, breaking the fine-china surface with crackling crunches.

About twenty feet beyond the barbershop lay a humble, two-story, shake-shingled building whose large, green-painted shingle over its front gallery identified it, in dark blue paint, as THE BLUE DOG SALOON. The storm doors were closed against the weather, of course, and Longarm could see no lights beyond the dark windows.

Judging by the lack of fresh hoofprints fronting the place, the Blue Dog was not a popular watering hole. But then, the lawman could see no fresh tracks of either man or beast anywhere in the street. Those he could see were partially filled in with windblown snow and were being covered gradually by the fresh stuff now coming down.

No horses or men were currently on the street or on the boardwalks or porches on either side of it. As he rode down the broad trace, heading toward one of the town's few side streets where he remembered the town constable's office was located, he thought he could see a couple of shadows moving in darkened windows. He was reasonably sure he saw a head move in a window of the Badlands Café as he passed the small white clapboard building on his left. He became certain sure when a hand reached through a checked gingham curtain to turn an OPEN sign around so that it now read CLOSED.

The hand was quickly withdrawn. The CLOSED sign danced briefly in its wake.

Longarm looked around warily, letting his trained lawman's eyes scan the buildings around him for signs of trouble. Something was definitely wrong here, he concluded. He hoped he'd find out what it was when he got to the constable's office and had a chat with Emmitt Grassley.

He turned the corner past Talbot's Tack and Feed and immediately saw that the constable's office, which was a small stone shack with a pitched wooden roof and sagging front gallery, was abandoned. The windows were dark, no smoke rose from the tin chimney pipe, and a small CLOSED sign hung from a sagging chain across the halved-log front door, near an empty wooden bird feeder jostling in the building wind.

A pristine snowdrift was piled beneath the feeder, in front of the door.

Longarm stopped his horse in front of the little stone building and looked around even more cautiously than before. Since it was the day after Christmas, it was no big surprise that Grassley wasn't manning his office. Longarm doubted that the crime rate in Little Missouri City dictated that the lawman be on hand at all or even most hours. But the fact of his absence—*prolonged absence*, judging by the unmolested snowdrift on the porch—accompanied by the downed telegraph wires and the suspicious movement in the windows along the main drag, only served to fuel Longarm's apprehension.

Seeing no immediate danger lurking among the shacks and stock pens around him, and recalling that the last time he'd been through here he'd had supper with Grassley and his wife in their house down by Little Missouri Creek, he touched heels to the Percheron's flanks. If Grassley wasn't in his office, he was probably at home. Longarm didn't think the man, who was middle-aged and none too ambitious, worked another job but merely tended chickens and a few cows now and then, which he fattened up over the summer and sold off at the beginning of every winter. Longarm remembered that the last time he was through this country, Grassley had been shacking up with a pretty mulatto woman maybe half Grassley's age.

Maybe he still was, though Longarm remembered thinking that the common-law marriage had seemed an odd one, the girl being pretty, Grassley being a middle-aged, borderline ne'er-do-well alcoholic.

Riding west of town and down a hill into a creek bottom, Longarm found the house where he'd remembered it—on a slight shelf built into the side of the creek's opposite bank. A nondescript, two-story log structure with a stable abutting its far right end, it was surrounded by scrub cedars, bur oaks, and cottonwoods. There was a second-story balcony of what appeared to be spindly planks and peeled log rails.

As Longarm climbed the hill via a two-track trail that was a faint purple line under the snow, the cabin's first-story door opened. The lawman could hear the squawk of the hinges beneath the growing wind and the rustling of the falling snow and creaking tree limbs.

A dark figure appeared in the dark doorway, and then Longarm saw the mulatto woman's chestnut face framed by wavy raven hair—and the big shotgun in her hands. As she stared out, a shawl nearly the same shade of red as Longarm's muffler wrapped around her head and spilling across her shoulders, she raised the shotgun across her chest and then canted her head to one side, scrutinizing her visitor.

Longarm waved as the Percheron approached. When he'd stopped the horse in front of the woman in the open door, he announced himself above the wind, and said, "I'm looking for the constable. Heard there was trouble in town. Something about dead lawmen."

The mulatto woman—oval-faced, smooth-skinned, with a fine broad nose and deep chocolate eyes—stared at him obliquely, caressing the shotgun's trigger guard with her bare right thumb.

"Is Grassley here?" Longarm asked, growing impatient.

"He's here," the woman said, jerking her head back to indicate the cabin's interior. "Stable your horse an' I'll show you to him."

Longarm neck-reined the Percheron over to the stable and dismounted outside the corral that ringed it. He opened the gate and led the big horse into the barn, carefully unsaddling and graining him, rubbing him down with burlap. He left the horse with a thick blanket over its back and then exited the stable, tapping softly on the cabin's front door as he entered, doffing his hat and untying his scarf.

The woman was tending a bubbling pot on the stove. She glanced at Longarm over her shoulder, then wiped her hands on her apron and said, "This way."

Longarm followed her down a hall that split the parlor area off from the kitchen, descended three steps into another short hall nearly as dark as night. The entire cabin was dark, with only stray wands of gray light penetrating through infrequent windows. On a brief expanse of wall hung an oil painting of a naked black woman sprawled leisurely across a red settee. The model had much darker skin than Grassley's wife. Longarm thought it odd to find the painting here when he'd seen so little else bedecking the cabin's walls, but he had more important questions on his mind.

The woman, whom Longarm guessed was in her late twenties or early thirties, rapped the back of a door with her knuckles, leaned close to the low, halved-log door, and said, "Hope you're decent. Comp'ny."

With that, she turned, her aloof, deep black eyes meeting Longarm's fleetingly, and then climbed the three steps to the kitchen, the floorboards creaking beneath her tread. Before Longarm could open the door, which she'd unlatched, a raspy male voice barked from the other side, "Another bottle, Bettina!"

The woman did not respond but merely disappeared into the shadows, the moccasins she was wearing scraping lightly across the floor.

Longarm had to duck low to step into the room. The air was so filled with cigar smoke that that he had to wave a hand in front of his face to catch a breath, his eyes stinging. "Grassley?" he said, choking on the word.

"Who's there?"

"Longarm."

"Long—?"

The man cut himself off, staring over his right shoulder at his visitor. The room was small and low-beamed, nearly barren except for the hide-bottom rocker in which the constable of Little Missouri City sat wrapped in a buffalo robe, a red stocking cap on his grizzled head. There was a low, three-shelf bookcase sagging with newspapers to his left, a sandbox to his right. The sandbox was so filled with the wrinkled brown worms of old cigars and gray ashes that no sand was visible. Grassley wore knit gloves on his stubby-fingered hands. An empty bottle and a half-empty glass stood atop an upended crate near the sandbox.

"Longarm," he said now, raspily, nodding slowly. His voice was slow, think, garbled. "I reckon Miss Jenny's telegram got through . . . just before them sons o' bitches cut the wires."

"What sons o' bitches?" Longarm asked.

"Ah, fuck!" the constable barked, lowering his head and kneading his forehead miserably with his left hand.

Chapter 11

Longarm walked up beside Grassley, but before he could repeat his question, the door opened behind him. Bettina walked in holding an amber bottle by its neck. She glanced at Longarm again in that oblique way of hers, picked up the empty bottle from the crate, replaced it with the fresh one, set another glass down beside Grassley's—presumably for Longarm—and left.

"Thank *you!*" Grassley yelled like a child recently scolded for impoliteness.

He picked up the bottle and popped the cork.

"The telegram got through, apparently," Longarm said. "I was over in Grand Forks. All the note said was that some lawmen had been killed here in Little Missouri City, and I was to investigate. Well, I'm here, investigatin', so if you wouldn't mind not taking another drink until you've filled me in, I'd appreciate that, old son!"

He grabbed the bottle away from the man, some of the whiskey sloshing out and dribbling down the side.

"Give me that, goddamnit! You got no right!"

"I got every right, Emmitt. Tell me what's happening in this town, where the killers are, and how many. Until you do, you won't be getting any more of your tangle-leg!"

"Ah, shit!" The constable ran a thick, knit-gloved hand down his face as though trying to scrub away several layers of skin. "I'm nothin' but a goddamn coward, Longarm!"

Longarm squatted down beside the chair, glared up at Grassley, and said sternly, "Tell me about the killers, Emmitt."

Grassley took a deep breath. "Jenny . . . she told me it's Emory Drake and two others from his bunch of high binders."

"Who's Jenny?"

"Tallant. Jenny Tallant. Runs the Blue Dog. Somehow, after Drake killed them lawmen, she snuck off to the telegraph office and had the station agent tap out a message to your office. She said Lew Patten told her to. Them was his last dyin' words. Ah, Christ, and here I sit, drunk an' gettin' drunker. Look at me!"

"Patten?" Longarm felt his guts recoil. "Lew Patten was one of the lawmen killed?"

"Yes, Patten." Grassley grabbed the bottle out of Longarm's hand. The federal lawman was too distracted by the tragic news of Patten's death to care about the whiskey. For all he cared, the cowardly constable could drink himself to death.

But not until after Longarm had gotten a few more answers.

As Grassley threw back another sizeable swallow of

the coffin varnish, Longarm dug the fingers of his right hand around the arm of the man's chair. He gritted his teeth. "Who else did the killers murder, Emmitt?"

"Federals," Grassley said when he finally lowered the bottle and scrubbed a grimy sleeve of his chenille robe across his mouth. "I didn't see 'em the day they was killed, but they and Patten had passed through town a few days before, on their way out to the Double Bar T Ranch out west. They was Brian Blake and Hoot Williams out of the Bismarck office. The Double Bar T foreman was with 'em—Sam Edwards."

Longarm nodded. He hadn't known the ranch foreman, but he'd met both of the federal lawmen. He hadn't known them as well as he'd known the older and more seasoned Sheriff Patten, but he'd known who they were. Both relatively young men. Both with families, Longarm believed. Wives, children . . .

Fury was a hot fire burning inside him.

Fellow lawmen murdered. One of those lawmen had been a good friend. Patten had been only a year or so from retirement. He'd intended to open his own saloon somewhere in Colorado, as he'd grown weary of the endless Dakota winters.

Longarm ground his fingers deeper into the chair arm. He was having trouble containing his rage at Emmitt Grassley for merely sitting here, getting drunk, and wallowing in self-pity while the killers of three lawmen ran free.

"Where are they, Emmitt?" he asked, trying to keep his voice even. "Where are them highbinders now?"

Grassley had just taken another hard pull from the bottle. When he'd finished swallowing and scrubbing his mouth again, he said, "Blue Dog, last I heard. Jenny said they was waitin' on the rest of their gang to show up. She thought they was headin' for a town south of here, to rob a bank or some such."

"When did you talk to this Miss Jenny?"

"A couple days ago. After the lawmen was killed. She come over to my office—told me all about it. Tried to get me to come over and see to things."

Tears rolled down Grassley's craggy, gray-bearded cheeks as he said, "I told her I'd have liked to have seen to them cross-grained bastards, but I just wasn't up to it. Shit, Longarm—that's Emory Drake over there! Drake and Curly Jenkins and Vincent McKirk! Why, shit, all three of them devilish bastards would just as soon kill a man as step around him in the street. Why, I've heard they'd shoot a lawman just to take target practice on his *badge!*"

"When's the last time you saw 'em?"

"Hell, I've *never* seen 'em. I told you, I wasn't about to walk over there! I told Jenny I was real sorry, but I just couldn't—"

"Emmitt, do you know if Drake and his pards are still over there? Maybe the rest of their gang showed up and they rode on."

Grassley just stared at Longarm for about five seconds, the man's face scrunched miserably. He seemed slow to comprehend what Longarm had just said, until he nodded twice and turned back to the bottle whose mouth he held level with his chin. "Could be, I reckon. I closed up the office and come over here"—he laughed in disgust at himself—"an' come over here right after Jenny left to go back into that lion's den. I told her to stay away, but she had to see about Miss Evangeline."

"Miss Evangeline?"

"The teacher. Leastways, that's what everybody around here calls her, since she used to be the school-teacher here. But ever since the school shut down, she's been workin' at the Blue Dog. You know—upstairs."

Longarm nodded his understanding. "Anyone else in there?"

"Shit, I don't know. Prob'ly just Jenny an' Miss Evangeline. Ain't seen nothin' of Jenny since the other day. Hell, she's probably dead. Same with the teacher."

"And here you sit," Longarm said, unable to contain his disdain for the man.

"And here I sit," Grassley said, sobbing and then raising the bottle to his lips once more. He lowered the bottle, swallowing and making a face against the burn, and turned to Longarm. "You'd be doin' me a favor if you shot me."

Longarm shook his head in disgust. "Yeah, well, your self-pity don't cut it, Emmitt. You can feel sorry for yourself all you want, but when I'm done over there at the Blue Dog, I'm gonna come back here and kick your stupid, cowardly ass."

"Shoot me!"

"That'd be too good for you." Longarm shook his head again as he turned and walked to the door. "No, I'll be back to kick your worthless ass and to take your badge away."

Drunkenly, Grassley sobbed again and spat out, "Fuck you, you son of a bitch!"

That last was muffled by the door that Longarm pulled closed behind him. He started for the kitchen but stopped abruptly. The woman, Bettina, stood at the bottom of the three steps, staring at Longarm. Obviously, she'd heard every word of his exchange with her husband.

"You going over there?"

Longarm shucked his Colt from its holster, flicked open the loading gate, and filled the chamber he always kept empty beneath the hammer with a shell from his belt. "Of course."

He closed the loading gate and spun the cylinder. It made a bee's whine.

"Storm's kickin' up," Bettina said. "Likely be a whiteout soon. Gettin' colder."

"Yeah, it won't be easy."

Longarm climbed the steps and walked to the front door, donning his hat and tying his scarf around his neck.

The woman followed him, saying, "He'd just be among the dead if he'd gone over there." She tossed her head to indicate the room that Longarm had just left.

He turned to her with one hand on the door handle. "How would that be any different from what he is now?"

He didn't wait for a response. He raised the collar of his coat and walked out into the storm.

Longarm saddled the Percheron and led the horse back out into the windblown snow. Bettina had been right. The storm was getting worse.

Waves of snow billowed, piling into drifts. The wind howled and moaned and the tree limbs creaked. The timbers of the cabin and barn screeched, the snow sounding like sand being thrown against the buildings. The horse balked but it was a dutiful mount, well trained by old Nikolai. When Longarm had climbed into the saddle and touched heels to the mount's flanks, it plodded back the way it had come—down into the creek bottom and up the other side.

Ahead, the buildings of the town looked ghostly gray behind the gauzy bridal veils of blowing snow.

Even the Percheron was having a hard time now, trudging through the freshly fallen stuff whipped into hard drifts. Longarm thought that as long as he could see a block or so ahead, he'd keep going. If visibility got any worse, he'd have to turn back. No point in getting lost in a whiteout. Having been lost in whiteouts before, he knew how easily it could happen. He'd heard of folks losing their way in such weather just trying to make it from their houses to their privies.

He crossed the intersection of the side street that the constable's office was on and the broader main street that was a gray field of blowing snow bordered on both sides by the gauzy gray figures of business buildings. Here, the wind had a clear route to him, and several icy gusts nearly blew him off his saddle. The Percheron shook its massive head and loosed a frustrated whinny.

Longarm continued pushing the Percheron to the mouth of an alley that he hoped trailed off to the rear of the Blue Dog on the north end of town. He swung down from the big horse's back and tied him to a hitchrack, the left leg of which was half-buried in fresh snow.

Northern plains blizzards were wicked bastards.

"Sorry, pal," Longarm told the horse, sliding his Winchester from the saddleboot. "If all goes well, I'll be back soon!"

He gave the Percheron's neck a pat, and, genuinely reluctant to leave the good horse in such foul weather but knowing horses like him were tougher than the usual saddle mount, he tramped off into the alley. He racked a shell into the Winchester's chamber, held the rifle up high across his chest, and lifted each knee nearly belt high as he plowed through the snow, heading in the direction of the Blue Dog Saloon.

It took him nearly fifteen minutes to bring up the two-story saloon ahead and on his right. He was breathing hard, his lungs burning from the cold, cold air. At least, he thought the building was the saloon he was looking for—a narrow, two-story barrack with a tall false facade. It fit the bill, though he couldn't see the green sign with blue letters from this angle. He thought he could see the much smaller building housing the barbershop just beyond it, however, so he stole cautiously toward the rear of the building in question.

It had a rear door under an outside stairs that climbed to another, second-story rear door.

Longarm had just started past the bottom of the stairs, heading for the first floor door, when he tripped on something yielding and fell to one knee and his right elbow. His knee and elbow had come down on the yielding thing that he knew just by feel was a body before he even looked to see that his elbow and knee had cleared snow away to reveal a fox fur coat that looked rather worn.

Longarm had seen plenty of dead bodies before, of

course. Still, touching one so unexpected-like wasn't his favorite thing to do, and he found himself recoiling a little. What was it about the absence of life that rendered a man so appalling?

Longarm quickly figured out which end was which and brushed snow away from the body's head to reveal a middle-aged face of a waxy hue. Two cobalt-blue eyes, glazed with death, stared up at him from beneath a wing of thick, black hair. A dark blue puckered hole had been drilled through his left cheek, just beneath that eye, which had swollen slightly and stared a little harder than the right one did. The bridge of the dead man's nose showed teardrop-shaped indentations, indicating he'd worn spectacles.

Longarm had brushed enough snow away to see that the dead man wore a preacher's collar. The lawman brushed a little more snow away to see two frozen, bloody wounds in the man's spindly chest, another in his belly. Maybe there'd been more folks in the saloon than Patten had thought. But what would a preacher be doing in a sin-soaked watering hole?

Noticing several more lumps in the snow beyond the dead preacher, Longarm brushed the dust away from two more and found that one of them was a dead deputy U.S. marshal out of Bismarck. The other was Lew Patten. His rage renewed, Longarm looked at the gray door to his left, a drift of snow rising two feet from the sill.

A muffled scream penetrated the saloon's rear wall. At least, Longarm thought it was a scream. Could have been a trick of the wind.

The scream sounded again. A woman's horrified outcry.

Hard thumps or bangs came from the saloon's second story. Just as Longarm raised his eyes to the second-story door, that door opened and a pale figure bounded out onto the stairs. A naked, full-bosomed figure. A girl's pale, naked figure!

She screamed as she dashed down from the top of the stairs that were liberally mounded with fresh snow. Longarm dropped his rifle and ran to the stairs, reaching the bottom just as the young woman's bare feet slipped out from beneath her. She screamed again, fell back onto the stairs, and yelped once more as she came rolling madly down the steps in a flurry of flying snow . . . and into Longarm's open arms.

At the same time, a man shouted from the top of the stairs.

A gun roared beneath the howling wind.

Chapter 12

The bullet hammered into the end of the stair rail well wide of Longarm and the naked girl, who'd fallen on top of him and was now writhing around, moaning as though they were making love out here in the blowing snow and howling wind, with someone shooting at them!

Longarm looked over the girl's brown-haired head to the top of the stairs where a red-haired gent wearing only red longhandles, socks, and a hat was stumbling drunkenly out onto the top landing, waving a pistol in his hand and bellowing angrily.

"Get back here, you fuckin' bitch!"

Just then the half-clad gent looked over the rail. His eyes found the girl and Longarm struggling together at the bottom of the steps. The redhead blinked as though to clear his vision. When he decided that his eyes were not deceiving him and that there really was a man down there with the girl, he gave a surprised, "What the *hell?*" and raised his pistol.

Longarm whipped up his own revolver, took hasty aim over the girl lying facedown atop him, and fired. The gun's roar was muffled by the wind. So was the underwear-clad gent's yelp as he triggered his own gun wild again and flew back through the open door behind him.

The bang of Longarm's gun had shocked the girl on top of him to silence. She glanced over her shoulder toward the top of the stairs, openmouthed, and then turned her horrified brown eyes on Longarm. She blinked and then screamed, *"Help me!"*

Longarm scrambled out from beneath the girl, keeping his eyes on the dark, menacing rectangle of the open door at the top of the stairs, and yelled, "Get up!"

The girl fumbled around on her hands and knees, full breasts jouncing. She was too cold and the snow was so slippery that she couldn't find a purchase.

Longarm cursed, looked back up at the open door. Seeing no one there, he quickly holstered his Colt, retrieved his rifle, and then grabbed one of the naked girl's flailing arms and drew her naked body up over his left shoulder.

She wailed with fright and, most likely, the torture of the penetrating wind and snow against her bare skin.

"Hold on, girl!" Longarm shouted, wheeling, holding the girl like a fifty-pound sack of cracked corn on his shoulder. "We're gonna get the hell out of here!"

Wrapping one arm over the girl's bare rump, he began to run back in the direction from which he'd come. It was a tough run in the deep snow, and his lungs complained against the fire of the cold air laced with falling snow. But he kept running, not sparing even a quarter of a second to look back to see if anyone was coming after him.

The girl cried and sobbed. She was as cold as a slab of pliant marble draped over Longarm's left shoulder. He had to get her to the only safe place he knew— Grassley's relatively remote cabin. He just hoped he made it before she froze to death, which wouldn't take long in this weather.

When he got back to the Percheron standing with its back covered with fresh snow, Longarm hastily brushed snow from the saddle and then tossed the naked girl up into it. He quickly slid his rifle into his saddle scabbard and then glanced back toward the saloon. Still finding no one coming after him, he unbuttoned and shrugged out of his coat.

The girl sat hunched and shivering on his cold, leather McClellan saddle.

"Here!" Longarm yelled, toeing a stirrup and then swinging up onto the Percheron's back behind her, awkwardly wrapping his coat around the girl's bare shoulders.

Her long brown hair blew out in the moaning wind. Leaning against her to keep the coat secured to her naked, shivering body, Longarm reined the big mount away from the hitchrack and rammed his heels against its flanks. He and the girl and the horse lumbered back along the side street through the snow that was piled up as high as the Percheron's knees.

As they crossed the broad main drag, Longarm looked to his right, toward the saloon, and then behind

him. He could still see no one following him. He didn't
know whether or not he'd killed the man on the stairs,
but he knew he'd at least grazed him. Still, according
to Patten, there were two more killers. Likely, the other
two were as drunk as the man Longarm had shot, and
would be slow to follow. The lawman hoped that by the
time they got around to trailing him and the girl, their
tracks would have been filled in by the wildly falling
snow.

Still, regardless of what condition any of the trio were
in, they knew he was here. Of course, they didn't know
who he was. But sooner or later, they'd come looking
for the man who'd taken the girl—unless Longarm ran
them down first.

"*Hi-yyahh, boy—goooo!*" he yelled at the Percheron
that was pitching and bounding through the snow, sending the downy flakes cascading up over Longarm's boots
and the girl's bare feet.

She crouched before him inside his coat, and he could
feel her shivering so badly that he had to hold her tightly
to keep her from falling off the horse.

The Percheron danced along the covered trail, following its own recent but faint tracks down into the
creek bottom and up the other side. As Longarm reined
up in front of the Grassley cabin, the door opened. Bettina stepped out holding a knit shawl over her shoulders.

"What on *earth?*" the woman called, scowling
through the dancing flakes at the all-but-naked woman
hunkered inside Longarm's coat. Hesitating for only a
second, she bounded out from cabin's front door and
ran around the hitchrack, reaching up toward the naked
girl, yelling, "Miss Evangeline—my *God!*"

Longarm leaped off the back of the Percheron, pulled the naked girl off his saddle and, with Bettina following only a step behind, carried her through the cabin's open door and set her down in a chair near the crackling fireplace. The girl—or young woman, Longarm saw, and a beautiful one at that, despite several cuts and bruises on her face—flopped back, only half-conscious, teeth clattering, her lips blue.

Longarm hesitated, not sure how to proceed. He had little experience with naked women he wasn't making love to. He was glad when Bettina shoved him aside, immediately dropping to her knees and going to work rubbing the blood back into the young woman's naked legs. Longarm's heavy, snow-dusted coat engulfed her.

"Where did you find her?" Bettina asked Longarm, breathless.

"I reckon she found me," the lawman said, grabbing a couple of split logs out of the woodbox flanking the fireplace and tossing both onto the grate, building up the fire. "She was running out of the saloon when I got there."

"I'm gonna need some more wood split," Bettina said.

"You got it."

"Take your coat. I'll get her warm."

Shrugging into his buckskin, Longarm swung toward the door. Bettina yelled behind him, "The woodshed's beyond the stable!"

Longarm went out and closed the door behind him. He stared through the thickly blowing snow toward the town. All he could see were the dancing curtains of the storm—like an Alberta Clipper—that had settled into

a furious frenzy over the town of Little Missouri City.
He doubted that any of the men from the saloon could
follow him and the girl here even if they wanted to. The
storm had grown too violent.

That meant he likely wouldn't make it back to the
saloon just now, either. He'd have to wait for a lull.

He turned to the horse standing slump-shouldered,
one hip cocked, at the hitchrack. The beast was cold
and tired. Longarm grabbed the reins and led the poor
animal through the corral and into the stable. Deciding
that he'd unsaddle his mount after he'd split some
wood—at least he had the horse in out of the storm—he
closed the doors behind him and headed for the wood-
pile sheltered by a rickety lean-to at the stable's far end.

He split a half-dozen cottonwood logs, wrapped the
wood in burlap for easier hauling, and carried it inside.
Bettina had laid a buffalo robe in front of the roaring
fireplace. The young woman, Miss Evangeline, sat on
the robe, knees to her chest, her back to the fire. She
had several blankets wrapped over her head and around
her shoulders. Her bare feet rested in a shallow pan of
steaming water. She held a steaming stone mug in her
hands.

She flinched when Longarm came in.

"Just me," he said, hauling the burlap bundle of wood
over to the large box beside the fireplace. "Name's Long.
I'm a deputy U.S. marshal." He dumped the wood into
the box. "You're Miss Evangeline?"

"Yes," the woman said, half-sullen, half-ironic, still
shivering inside all those blankets. "I'm the one they
call the teacher."

Bettina came into the kitchen, stirring something in

a mug with a small wooden spoon. She dropped to both knees beside Miss Evangeline.

"Turn to me," Bettina said, dipping her fingers into the mug and beginning to gently smear the paste, which smelled like warm mushrooms but was probably some healing concoction made from roots and herbs, into a four-inch gash running across the nub of the teacher's left cheek, beneath her lightly swollen, discolored eye.

Miss Evangeline groaned but held her face still while Bettina continued to rub the salve into the cut.

Longarm brushed the sawdust from his pants, removed his gloves and mittens, and dropped to a knee on the other side of Miss Evangeline from Bettina. Vaguely, he was aware of snores rising from the back of the house, which would be Constable Grassley, sound asleep.

"Pretty bad over there?" Longarm asked the teacher.

"Yes," she said, wincing against Bettina's ministrations. "It's pretty bad." She turned to Longarm, looked him up and down. "Are you alone, Marshal Long?"

"Yes, he is," Bettina answered for him in a tone that conveyed her disgust for her drunken, passed-out husband. "He's all alone."

"I do appreciate your help," the teacher said. "They tied me to my bed with a torn-up sheet, but I worked one of the strips free. When I heard one of them coming up the stairs, I didn't even bother to throw anything on, but just left my room and ran to the nearest door. If you hadn't been at the bottom of those steps, I'd be dead. Either shot or frozen. Probably both."

"Well, you're safe now."

"Those bastards," Bettina said, rubbing the salve into

a deep bruise on the teacher's right cheek. "I hope they feel like real, tough men!"

"There's three of them?" Longarm asked. "Drake, Jenkins, and McKirk?"

"There were three," the teacher said. "I heard some shooting yesterday. Now I think there may only be two—Drake and Jenkins. But there's a girl there now. A stranger. They hauled her up to the room next to mine, and they're giving her the same working over that they'd been giving me. Just before I left, they dragged her downstairs and forced her to play the piano."

"Where'd she come from?"

Miss Evangeline merely shook her head. Bettina looked at him. Enough questions. The teacher was exhausted from the beating she'd taken in the saloon and from her ordeal with Longarm out in the weather.

"I'm gonna tend my horse," he said.

"I'll fry us up some steaks," Bettina said as Longarm strode to the door.

"Not for me," he said, glancing back at her. "I'm not hungry."

"You gotta eat somethin'," Bettina told him. Finished coating the teacher's face with the healing salve, she was adjusting the blankets over the young woman's shoulders. "Besides, the storm's tearin' up like a Loo-zee-anna hur'cane. By the looks of it, this'll continue all night. Might clear up by mornin'."

"All right." Frustrated, Longarm went back out into the storm. He looked around the cabin, but did not see any fresh tracks that were not his own.

Satisfied that none of the killers had followed him, he trudged through the deep snow to the stable and again tended the trusty Percheron. That chore accomplished, he took his rifle, saddlebags, and bedroll, and returned to the cabin. Bettina was filling the cabin with the aroma of frying beef, potatoes, and onions. Instantly, Longarm was hungry.

He stowed his gear on the floor near the door, shook the snow off his coat and hat, and hung both on pegs over his gear. Then he sat at the table from which, through a window, he had a good view of the front yard and the trail leading to the creek bottom and town, and he rested his Winchester across his thighs. He'd noted when he'd come in that Miss Evangeline was no longer sitting by the fire. Bettina must have put her to bed, where she'd likely sleep the rest of the day and night.

It was just Longarm and Grassley's young mulatto wife in the kitchen. Longarm could still hear Grassley's muffled snores emanating from the back room.

Bettina dished up Longarm a steak that overhung its large platter, and topped it with buttery friend potatoes and onions. She dished up a smaller portion for herself and then sat down across from him, and they ate in silence. The grub was perfectly cooked and tasty, and when Longarm was finished, he was full to bursting.

"Much obliged," he said.

Bettina smiled at him with her large brown eyes, and then she removed his dishes, replaced them with a water glass and a bottle. The label on the bottle identified it as TOM MOORE'S MARYLAND RYE—Longarm's drink of choice since his very first sip more years back than he cared to remember.

He looked at Bettina questioningly. She was coming back from the kitchen with a handful of cheap cigars

and a water glass for herself, her hips working beautifully inside her tight-fitting cotton dress. Her large eyes
were glued to him, her wide mouth quirking in a beguil-
ing smile. Flames from the fire danced in her eyes.

"That's what you drink, isn't it?" she asked as she sat
down across from. "I remembered from the last time
you were through here. Smoke these, too, don't ya?"

She tossed the cigars down onto the middle of the
oilcloth-covered table.

Longarm just gazed at her, one brow arched. In the
back room, Grassley continued to snore.

"You gonna open that bottle?" she said. "Or am I
gonna have to open it for you?"

Chapter 13

An hour earlier, Miss Jenny had stood mesmerized behind the bar at the Blue Dog Saloon, watching the girl, whoever she was—the one who'd come in with the now-dead Preacher, or whatever *he'd* been—play the piano abutting the far wall.

The girl seemed to be in a state of shock after what Drake and Jenkins had done to her upstairs, getting even for the Preacher killing McKirk. Even in the numb state she appeared to be in, the girl's pale hands fairly floated across the piano's yellowed ivory keys, kicking out sounds that Jenny, in all her years running the Blue Dog, had never heard it turn loose before.

The girl was not playing the familiar old ditties and jigs. No, she was playing what even Miss Jenny's untutored ears recognized as European music.

Classical music, she thought it was called.

The piano was badly out of tune. Still, the notes seemed to float off the girl's hands like little melodic

birds to dance in the air and fill the room, still rife with
the smells of blood, death, and powder smoke, with
sublimity.

While Miss Jenny was taken with the soft, pretty
music, she kept shuttling her gaze toward where Drake
and Jenkins sat at the same table they'd been occupying
for the past three days—between trips upstairs to Miss
Evangeline or the new girl, that is. Drake was passed
out, snoring, his head resting on his folded arms on the
table. He sat on the far side of the table from Jenny, the
top of his head facing the proprietor of the Blue Dog.

Jenkins faced his partner, his back to Jenny. Jenkins
was fighting sleep induced by all the whiskey they'd
drunk so far that day—at least a bottle and a half each,
Jenny thought. The girl's music was also acting like a
tonic on them. It was filing the edges off their nasty,
jangled nerves, putting them both to sleep.

Jenkins's head was just now tipped far back on his
shoulders, nose tipped to the ceiling, mouth wide open,
his playing cards clutched in his right hand. His chin
drooped ever so slowly toward the table, moving herkily-
jerkily as the man fought the sleep threatening to over-
come him.

Meanwhile, the girl's gentle hands continued to float
across the chipped ivory keys, causing the little birds of
the music to chirp and pipe as they careened from one
end of the smoky, dusky room to the other. As the girl
played, Jenny's heartbeat quickened anxiously.

She caressed the edge of the polished bar with her
fingers as she stared at the walnut grips of the revolver
jutting from the holster resting against Jenkins's right
thigh. The gun sat nearly parallel to the floor, the grips

facing out behind the man, beneath his right elbow. If Jenny could make it over to the table without either man hearing her, she should be able to pull the gun out of the holster and shoot both Jenkins and Drake before either rapist and killer knew what was happening.

Jenkins's head sagged down close to the table. His freckled forehead was nearly on the table itself when he grunted and jerked his head up sharply.

Jenny winced.

Jenkins shook his head, smacked his lips, and raked his left hand down his face. He frowned, bleary-eyed, across the table at his unconscious partner, and then he spread the cards in his right hand, leaning forward to scrutinize the pasteboards through the screen of all the whiskey he'd consumed.

Jenny looked at the girl, silently encouraging her to keep playing. She'd been playing for about fifteen minutes and didn't look to be in any hurry to stop. Her hands kept fluttering over the keys.

The bittersweet little birds kept flying, chirping above the regular moaning of the wind outside, and the ticking of the blowing snow against the windows and walls.

Absently, Jenny wondered where the girl had learned to play like that. At one time she must have had a right fancy family who could afford such niceties. Now, here she was, out in the middle of cold-assed nowhere, in the coldest town in hell, playing such fine, pretty tunes after she'd been so violated by the two brigands at the far table.

Jenny returned her gaze to the brigands of topic.

Just as she did, Jenkins groaned a half second before he let his head, appearing to be as heavy as lead, finally sink down onto his crossed arms. Jenny's heart fluttered, hiccupped. Her mouth dried. She ran her tongue over her chapped lower lip and rubbed her hands on her overall-clad thighs. She looked from Jenkins to Drake, who was snoring beneath the pattering of the piano, and back to Jenkins, who also started snoring.

Jenny turned and walked slowly out from behind the bar. She stared at the killers' table littered with coins, paper money, dirty glasses, and a nearly empty whiskey bottle. Jenny had been removing their empty bottles and emptying their ashtray, or else they'd be virtually buried under the refuse of their debauchery.

Silently willing the girl to keep playing, Jenny walked toward the killers' table. She kept nervously rubbing her hands on her overall slacks, silently praying that the brigands would keep sleeping. As she approached their table, their snoring grew louder.

Anxiety caused every nerve in Jenny's large, fleshy body to twist and leap.

She drew within six feet of the table. The alcohol and tobacco stench of the pair nearly made her eyes water— quite a feat for a longtime saloon owner. The steel band running down the end of the handle of Jenkins's Schofield .44 grew larger and larger in Jenny's staring eyes. She took another step and began extending her hand toward the gun.

She looked at Drake, who continued to snore, red-faced, slack-jawed, on his arms. He pooched out his lips with every exhalation.

She looked at Jenkins. She could see only the back of his head. He wasn't wearing his hat and his wool-like

curly hair was oily and flecked liberally with dandruff.
Jenny had seen cleaner buffalo hides.

She reached toward the steal-banded grips of the man's
revolver. Her heart was fairly racing now, drumming in
her ears so that she could just barely hear the girl's piano
playing. Already, in her imagination, Jenny had the gun
out and was aiming it at Jenkins's filthy head.

Bang!

The man's head hadn't quit jerking before Jenny
aimed the pistol at Drake, drew the hammer back,
and . . . *BANG!*

Both men, dead.

Jenny's troubles over . . .

Jenny heard herself gasp on the heels of the horrify-
ing click of a revolver hammer being drawn back to full
cock. She raised the hand that she'd been about to close
around the grips of Jenkins's pistol and slid it over the
table, shifting her gaze to the pistol that Drake was aiming at her from two feet away. The man, his eyes rheumy
and red and pink-rimmed, stared up at Jenny as the
saloon proprietor picked up two empty shot glasses with
just her right thumb and index finger, and scowled at
the killer aiming the gun at her.

"Get the hump out of your neck," she said, the calm-
ness of her tone belying the frustrated screaming in her
ears and the continuing pounding of her heart. "Just trying to keep up with all the dirty dishes you fellas are
leavin'." She tried to ignore Drake's cocked pistol and
maintain a calm expression, an even tone. "You want
another bottle? At the rate you're goin', that one'll be
empty in no time."

Jenkins grunted and lifted his head with a start, blinking up at Jenny. He appeared dazed, confused.

"Mind your gun," Drake raked out at him, grinning knowingly up at Jenny. "It damn near got this ugly old hag riddled so full of lead she'd have rattled when she walked."

Jenkins dropped his right hand to his gun, frowning.

Jenny frowned, sighed. To Drake, she said, "Mister, I haven't fired nothin' but an old shotgun for nigh on as long as you've walked this earth. I wouldn't even know how to shoot a pistol. Maybe you best slow up with the who-hit-john. I think your thinker box is gettin' mushy."

She knew she'd been pushing it with the back talk, but her nerves had gotten away from her. She swung around and began ambling back to the bar, gooseflesh rising across her shoulders, knowing that there was a good chance Drake would shoot her there. When he did not, and she found herself behind the bar again, she assumed he'd let her live only because he enjoyed being cooked for and served, his ashtrays emptied, depleted bottles carted away.

Jenny had a feeling that if the rest of his gang ever showed up, and she was no longer useful to him, he'd take his leave of her by first drilling a bullet between her eyes.

The girl kept playing the piano as though oblivious to what had just transpired.

"Ah, hell," Jenkins said, pushing heavily to his feet. "I'm gonna go up and get me another poke and take a nap with that big-titted teacher."

Jenny watched, crestfallen and trying not to sob, as the redhead stumbled away from the table and began pounding heavily up the stairs. Drake grinned know-ingly at Jenny once more, holstered his pistol, and began absently shuffling the cards in his hand.

Jenny had just poured herself a calming drink when Jenkins gained the top of the stairs and started shout-ing. Jenny's heart hiccupped again when she heard Miss Evangeline scream. Bare feet pounded the second-story floor over Jenny's head.

Jenkins shouted again. Drake shouted then, too, and pushed himself to his feet to run toward the stairs, but he tripped over a chair and dropped to his knees with a curse.

The running sounds continued in the ceiling over Jenny's head.

Miss Evangeline screamed again, though it was more muffled this time, as though she'd gotten outside.

Jenkins shouted. A pistol popped.

"Oh, dear God," Jenny said, taking a deep, calming breath and raising her drink to her lips in a quivering hand. "Oh, dear God—what now?"

Meanwhile, the strange girl kept releasing the little silver-winged birds from the yellow keys of the Blue Dog's bullet-pocked piano.

Chapter 14

Longarm threw back the last of a half glassful of Maryland rye, sighed in satisfaction of the heart-warming, familiar elixir, which soothed him clear down to his toes, and took a deep drag off his second three-for-a-nickel cheroot of the stormy afternoon. He turned to the window, blowing the smoke out against the frosty glass.

He studied the storm for a time while he finished the cigar. Stubbing the cheroot out in the ashtray that Bettina had provided, he rose and reached for his coat.

"Where you goin'?" Bettina asked on the other side of the table from him, holding her own empty glass in both hands beneath her chin. Her eyes were a little glassy from the rye.

They hadn't talked much during the past hour. Longarm had too much on his mind for small talk. It had been nice to sit here with Grassley's woman, however. Bettina had been a quiet, soothing, companionable presence. The only sounds had been the storm outside and her husband's snores emanating from the rear of the cabin.

Longarm turned to the window again as he buttoned his coat. "Looks like it might have lightened a little. I'm gonna check it out."

Bettina came around the table and dipped her chin to look through a relatively clear spot in the glass. "That's wishful thinkin'."

"Nevertheless," Longarm said, wrapping his scarf around his neck, "I'm gonna check it out. If it's clear enough for me to make it into town, it's clear it enough for them killers in the Blue Dog to make it out here."

Bettina just stared at him with those lustrous brown eyes of hers and turned her mouth corners down. Longarm picked up his rifle, racked a round into the chamber, off-cocked the hammer, and went out to where the wind threatened to snatch his hat off his head. Drawing the Stetson down tighter and keeping his head low, he strode out away from the cabin, pushing through a deep drift that had curled up against the hitchrack. Once past the drift, the going was a little easier, the snow feathering away from just above his knees.

Longarm walked out to the edge of the yard and started down into the gulley through which the creek twisted. The gully was as white as a wedding cake, the columns of the cottonwoods and box elders standing out black against it. The wind was stronger here. The blue, blowing snow stung his cheeks like miniature javelins. His eyes grew sticky from jelling tears. The snow rose to his thighs, and it grew deeper the farther he dropped into the ravine.

Still he trudged on down the grade.

Something moved ahead of him—a dark figure shifting suddenly.

Longarm raised the rifle to his shoulder, instantly thumbing back the hammer. A moment later, he eased the tension in his trigger finger. The wind had dislodged a large tuft of snow from the V between two branches about midway up a tall, sprawling cottonwood standing on the creek's opposite bank.

As his heart slowed, he off-cocked the hammer and lowered the Winchester to his side. He looked around carefully, spying no tracks or even the sign of tracks that had been recently filled in by the wind and snow. His and the Percheron's tracks from earlier were gone without a trace.

The weary but determined lawman continued down to the bottom of the creek, where he nearly had to swim through the snow. As he made for the opposite ridge, he fell twice and had a devil of a time getting up. The snow was like a giant tub of frigid goose down.

Longarm stopped near the big cottonwood, which he leaned against, bending slightly forward at the waist, catching his breath. His heart thudded against the strain of the hard trek. He stared toward town. All he could see of Little Missouri City was a vague shifting outline of purple denoting the buildings beyond the thick, buffeting veils of blowing snow.

The wind was so strong out here that it threatened to blow Longarm back into the ravine.

He could see now that he'd been wrong. From the cabin's window, the storm might have appeared to be letting up, but it wasn't. Not by a long shot. If he tried hard enough, he might be able to make it into town, but it was likelier he'd get turned around in the storm and lose his way, or flounder in the deep snow and get stranded, only to freeze to death. Even if he made it to the saloon, would he have enough energy left for confronting Lew Patten's killers?

As it was, he could no longer feel his fingers or his toes or the nubs of his cheeks. His eyes were stinging; they felt as though they were turning to ice in their sockets. No point in pushing this hard. He'd wait for a true lull, and then he'd venture on to the Blue Dog and give the rapists and killers their just desserts.

He turned around and began retracing his steps. It took him nearly a half hour to make it back to the cabin. His feet were frozen; they felt like lead. He gave the front door a single knock, announcing himself, and it came open before he could trip the latch himself. He stumbled inside on a wave of blowing snow and fell to one knee.

"Oh!" Bettina intoned with a start, closing the door behind him. "I told you—didn't I?"

"What the hell are you doin'?" asked a raspy, slurred voice.

Still on one knee, catching his breath, Longarm doffed his hat and looked up. Emmitt Grassley stood clinging to a ceiling support post back in the cabin's shadows, his chenille robe loosely tied around his pot-bellied frame clad in grubby longhandles. His thin hair hung in his eyes, which he blinked several times, trying to focus.

"What the fuck's it look like?" Longarm wheezed out at the man. He glanced at Bettina sheepishly. "Pardon my French."

"Don't hold your tongue on my account," Bettina said with a grunt as she helped Longarm to his feet and then eased him down into the same chair he'd been sitting in before.

"Get away from him—goddamn you, woman!" Grassley yelled, waving an arm as he slogged forward, pushing off furniture to keep from falling. "She wants you," he told Longarm, flaring his nostrils angrily. "I can smell it on her!"

Longarm glanced at Bettina. She said only, "Best get out of them boots. I'll fetch a pan of warm water, thaw you out."

"I'm hungry!" Grassley yelled, holding on to a chair back and glaring at his wife.

"Sit down, then," Bettina said, filling a pan from a wooden pail hanging near the dry sink.

Grassley slacked into the chair across from Longarm, staring at the federal lawman with unconcealed disdain. "Fool's move," he said. "Headin' out in weather like this."

Longarm kicked out of his left boot, gritting his teeth against the pain in the half-frozen appendage. "What should I do? Stay here and get drunk and wallow in cowardice and self-pity?" Grassley was such a mean drunk—something Longarm hadn't known about him before—that he deserved such insults. The man wasn't only a self-pitying coward, but a cruel one. Longarm had no more time for the man.

Grassley poured out a couple of fingers of the Maryland rye, glowering and muttering curses. Meanwhile, as Longarm kicked out of his other boot, Bettina produced a filled plate from the range's warming rack and set it on

the table before her husband, with a napkin and silver-
ware. She refilled Longarm's glass, corked the bottle, and
removed it from the table.

"Hey, where you goin' with that?" Grassley groused.
"You've had enough!"

"Goddamnit, woman!" The constable heaved himself
out of his chair, staggered into the parlor area of the
front cabin, reached behind a bookshelf, and grinned
superiorly as he pulled out a half-filled, unlabeled brown
bottle. He popped the cork, took a hefty pull of the bust-
head, smacked his lips with exaggeration, and staggered
back over to the table, setting the fresh bottle down pro-
prietarily close to his plate.

"That stuff gonna kill you, you damn fool," Bettina
berated him as she set a pan of warm water on the floor
near Longarm. To the federal lawman, she said,
"There—set your feet in that. Tell me if it's too hot.
Should only be lukewarm, not hot." She sucked a breath
and shook her head, looking up at him from beneath her
black brows. On her knees, she leaned forward slightly,
causing her dress and cream-colored chemise to open,
giving Longarm a clean view of her full brown breasts
sloping out away from her chest. He could see clear down
to her large brown nipples, which appeared swollen.

He tried to look away too late. She'd caught the direction of his glance, looked down at her open dress, and
her cheeks blanched slightly, though her lips also
quirked a fleeting, knowing half smile.

"That's fine," Longarm said, feeling his ears warm
with chagrin as he dipped his bare feet into the water.
"That's perfect. Much obliged, Bettina."

She met his gaze again, and, doing nothing to prevent

another look down her dress, she straightened slowly, walked over to fill a plate from a skillet on the range, poured coffee into a stone mug, muttered something about checking on the teacher, and disappeared through a curtained doorway.

"Bettina, is it?" Grassley was glaring over the top of his bottle, breathing loudly through his nose—a phlegmy, drunken wheeze. "Got to know her right well over the past coupla hours."

Longarm ignored the accusation. Instead, he picked up one of the cheroots Bettina had laid out for him, scratched a match to life on the table, and lit the cigar. Smoke wafted in the dingy air around him. He blew out a long plume of smoke at Grassley, who blinked and coughed, and then Longarm said, "How many more is Drake waiting on?"

Grassley coughed again, waved the smoke away from his face, picked up his fork and knife, and started cutting into his steak. "A lot. He's got a lot ridin' for him. That's all I know. That's all I *care* about knowin'."

"What in the hell are you wearin' a badge for?"

"All I know is that every one of 'em is as crafty with a shootin' iron as Drake himself is. They're no bunch to mess with."

"Answer my question."

"Here!" The constable slammed his knife and fork down on the table, fished out his tin badge, which appeared to have been cut from the lid of a tin can, and threw it onto the middle of the table. The wan light from a lantern and a couple of burning candles shone on it dully. "There you go. There's my badge, federal man. It's all yours."

Longarm stared at the pathetic man before him as he took another deep drag off his cigar. This time he exhaled the smoke toward the parlor area that was mostly in shadow despite the fire and a lit red lantern atop the fireplace mantel. The storm continued to scream around the cabin like hysterical witches, causing the timbers to creak and the fire in the hearth to wheeze and puff.

"What the hell you intend to do, Custis?" Grassley asked, chewing. "You intend to take on Drake and his whole gun-savvy gang *yourself?*"

"That looks to be the size of it," Longarm said caustically.

Grassley was so pie-eyed and downtrodden that he didn't even seem embarrassed by the barb. "Then you're a damn fool. I may be a coward, but you're a damn fool. They don't pay you enough to go into a rattlesnake nest the size and shape of that one over there!"

"No, they don't," Longarm agreed mildly. "But I agreed to wear the badge for what they do pay me, and that means that when I find myself in a situation like this, possibly facing down an entire gang of fork-tailed desperadoes, then, by God, that's what I do. If law enforcement was loaded up with men like you, Emmitt, there'd be damned few laws being enforced."

Grassley stopped chewing. That seemed to have punched through his mushy hide. He glared with his chin down low. "I don't have to take that from you. Not in my own house, I don't!"

"Yes, you do." This from Bettina, who'd just stepped back through the curtained doorway with Miss Evangeline's empty plate. She stared dully down at her husband, too appalled by the man's behavior to even show it any-more. She just looked sad and tired and worn-out.

Grassley switched his glare to his wife. He looked her up and down, nostrils flaring. "Smell it on ya! I can just smell it on ya!"

With that, he pushed up from the table. He must have gotten a leg tangled up with his chair, because he fell forward and had to catch himself with both hands, turn-ing the bottle over. He swiped up the bottle before much whiskey could spill out of it, then turned his pugnacious gaze back to Longarm. "If you're gonna fuck my whore, you leave your money on the table. Right here!"

He hammered knuckles against the table's scarred surface. He grinned lasciviously at his wife. Bettina stared levelly back at him, expressionless. Snarling and clutching the bottle to his chest, Grassley stumbled out away from the table and staggered, tripping over scatter rugs, down the steps and into the shadows at the back of the cabin.

Outside, an unusually violent gust of wind slammed the cabin so hard that all the walls and ceilings whined like a wounded animal, and a log fell from the fireplace grate with a loud thud, sparking.

Chapter 15

"I'm sorry," Bettina said, dropping the dishes into the dry sink. "About him—Emmitt. I'm sorry."

"Don't worry about it. He's in his own hell."

"Well, I reckon he put himself there, didn't he?" she said, clearing her husband's dishes from the table. "You want some coffee, or just the rye?"

"I reckon I'd better have some coffee to go with the rye."

When Bettina had finished brewing the coffee, she poured a cup for Longarm, and he emptied his whiskey glass into his coffee cup and stirred the sweet-smelling concoction with a spoon. She finished cleaning the kitchen, and then they sat together at the table, Longarm sipping his coffee and rye and staring out the window, his rifle resting across his knees. Grassley's snores were soon emanating again from his room.

Several times throughout the afternoon, Bettina left the kitchen to check on Miss Evangeline and to take tea to the battered woman.

The storm continued howling as though it would go on howling for the next hundred years. The night closed down early.

When there was only a little gauzy light left, Longarm put on his socks, boots, hat, and coat and headed out to the barn to tend the Grassleys' stock and his borrowed Percheron. When he'd finished the chores, he split enough wood to keep the fires going throughout the night and the next day, making several trips to haul it all inside. Bettina built up the fire in both the fireplace and the range and made supper—steak and beans with garden greens that Longarm figured she'd put up herself, and dried apricot pie and coffee for dessert.

Around eight, after she'd taken supper to the ex-teacher, she banked the fire in the hearth and turned to Longarm. "I'm going to hit the hay. It's been a long day."

Sitting at the kitchen table, Longarm was lighting another cheroot. "Thanks for all the food and hard work."

Bettina did not respond to that but rolled her eyes over to the stairs rising on the far right side of the kitchen. The stair rail was composed of unpeeled pine logs draped with colorful Indian blankets. "There's a room up there. There's no heat, but I've added an extra quilt to the bed."

"Thanks," Longarm said, "but I reckon I'd best stay up."

"This storm won't start to die till after sunup. I've lived up here on these plains long enough to know how it is. Those men won't come out here. You've had a long day yourself, Marshal Long. Best go on to bed, get a good night's sleep. I reckon you're gonna need it tomorrow."

With that, she turned and disappeared into the darkness at the back of the cabin. Longarm heard her go into a room separate from the one in which Grassley was still snoring, waking up occasionally only to snort and grunt and drink himself unconscious again. Her door latch clicked. Longarm felt a heaviness in his belly. He'd liked it better when she was out here, even if she did belong to another man.

He turned to the window and continued to smoke and listen to the wind thrash the place with snow. He kept imagining a God-sized creature hovering out there in the darkness, tossing one giant fistful of snow after another at the cabin. His eyelids grew heavy.

Bettina was right. He should go to bed. Nothing more was going to happen until the storm blew itself out.

Longarm walked out onto the stoop and evacuated his bladder in the large drift that had all but buried the hitchrack. The wind was so cold it damn near froze his pecker before he could empty himself of all the whiskey and coffee he'd drunk.

Back inside, he blew out the lamps and most of the candles but took one of the candles embedded in a coffee tin filled with sand up to the room in the second story. The storm sounded even worse up here. The room's door had been open to the heat rising from below, so it wasn't uncomfortably cold.

He kept the door open about a foot, undressed, and crawled into the bed. The coarse sheet and heavy quilts felt good. They felt better as they trapped his own musky heat inside them, wrapping him in it. The covers smelled like Bettina, and this troubled him for a brief time, prodding his loins and causing him to remember the fullness of her breasts with their swollen nipples sloping out from her chest when she'd been kneeling before him earlier.

The whiskey and the howling wind made short work of him, however, and he tumbled off into oblivion. But only for a short time. He woke to the creaking of the stairs outside his room. A watery light grew beyond the gap he'd left in the door. And then a dark figure followed the light through the door. Bettina set the lamp on the dresser, turned toward the bed, and shrugged out of the blanket that was all she'd been wearing.

"He's no man to me," she said huskily, holding the lamp up high beside her. The amber-yellow light bathed her beautifully, stretching the shadows of her deep, full breasts down her side and across the floor to her left.

"No," Longarm said, shaking his head. He couldn't take a man's woman in the man's own home. Despite the pathetic coward that Emmitt Grassley had turned out to be, he couldn't take the man's wife under Grassley's own roof.

Bettina raised the light higher, shrinking the dark shadows beneath her breasts, bathing the beautiful brown orbs in a rich honey luminescence. The nipples were pebbled, distended. The breasts themselves rose and fell as she breathed, her lips parted slightly.

"You don't want me?" she said. "You gonna turn me away, Longarm?"

"Ah, Christ."

She stepped closer to the bed. "Look at me," she said, keeping her voice low. "He ain't no man to me." She took Longarm's hand, held it to her full, firm right tit,

pressed the tip of his index finger against the hard, jutting nipple. "He hasn't been a man to me since the who-
hit-john took him over. Three years now. He won me in
a poker game when I was fifteen. Fifteen. But he ain't
never really been a man to me. He thought he could treat
me like shit because my momma—she was a whore in
the French Quarter, New Orleans."

That must have been the black woman in the painting downstairs, Longarm absently reflected.

"He ain't no man to me, Longarm." She flicked his
finger across her jutting nipple. "Be a man to me, Longarm." She looked down at his large, weathered hand on
her tit and closed her upper teeth over her bottom lip.
"It's cold out here."

Longarm knew that what he was about to do was
wrong, but he couldn't deny her. He couldn't deny himself. He pulled the covers back off him and started
unbuttoning his longhandles. His cock stood up tall and
rigid, having found its own way through the fly of his
longhandles. It arced back over his belly, jerking with
each thud of his heart. Bettina closed her hand over it.
The room was chilly. Her hand was warm. She caressed
him gently, sending shocks of erotic bliss into every
fiber of his being while he shucked out of his underwear.

As she manipulated him with her hand, she pressed
her lips to his belly. He could feel the warmth of her
mouth, the wetness of her tongue. Pumping him a little
harder now, she ran her tongue slowly up from his belly
button toward his chest. As she did, she crawled in
beside him and pulled the covers over them both.

Her hand was warm, gentle. Longarm's blood rose.

Outside, the storm continued to batter the cabin, moaning and groaning like some lost demon trying to find its way back to hell.

Straddling him, Bettina pressed her warm snatch with its tangle of black hair against his cock. She wrapped her arms around his neck and kissed him hungrily, her moans nearly drowned by the storm. She slipped her tongue into his mouth, and he entangled it in his own, wrapping his arms around her, lowering his hands to knead her firm, round ass, causing her to groan louder.

He lowered his hands still farther, found her furred mound, and slipped two fingers inside.

She lifted her head, squeezed her eyes shut, and moaned louder as he continued to fuck her with his fingers.

After they kissed and grunted around for a time, Bettina reached down between them for his cock. She scuttled down the broad, brawny length of him, sucked the head of his hard-on for a while, lubricating it up good with saliva, and then slipped it into her pussy. She cried out as the swollen mushroom head hit bottom, and sat up straight atop him, throwing her long, curly black hair behind her shoulders.

She leaned forward slightly, clutching the slabs of his pectorals, and began to rise up and sink down on his cock. Longarm groaned as her wet snatch engulfed him over and over again. Her prickly hair scratched him delightfully. She quickened her pace, and it was only a minute or two before she was riding him hard, almost painfully, crouched over him now and sinking her teeth into his shoulder as her pretty brown ass bobbed on his crotch.

She came quickly, her juices dribbling down around him, pressing her thighs hard against him, viselike, and mashing her big tits against his chest.

"Oh," she said when she'd stopped spasming. "Oh, God—that was fuckin' *wonderful!*"

Bettina laughed deep in her throat, kissed him vigorously, nibbled his lips, and then rested her head on his chest for a time. Longarm had not yet come, and his hard cock was still standing up firm in her womb. She seemed to like that, smiling and moving her pussy around on him slightly, teasingly, as she rested luxuriously against his chest.

Those little movements prodded him gently at first, but soon his blood was boiling. He placed his hands on the firm, round globes of her ass again. She laughed at that, sensing his growing urgency. He sucked her tits, lapping each nipple in turn while she groaned and writhed. Then he pushed himself up onto his right shoulder, easily rolling her onto her back. He slid his arms up under her thighs and lifted her knees nearly to her ears, mounting her good and proper.

"Oh, fuck!" she intoned, laughing delightedly. "Oh, fuck me!"

Propped on his outstretched arms, fists buried in the pillow on either side of her head, Longarm began thrusting hard but slowly. He gradually increased his speed, his cock feeling like one large exposed nerve filled with lightning, until he was slapping his hips against her loudly and she was by turns screaming and mewling with desire. She dug her fingers into his ass, ground her heels into his sides, and flopped and bounced as he rode her.

Bettina's pussy grabbed at him, contracting and expanding.

Faster and faster and harder and harder he pummeled her . . . until they both came at the same time.

Longarm could not stifle a deep, guttural groan of fulfilled desire.

She gave one of her own, which he hoped like hell could not be heard above the storm, though he figured, judging by the volume of the echoes around the room, that that was too much to hope for.

They lay entangled and unmoving for about five minutes. Then she wiggled around beneath him, grunting. He rolled onto his back. She turned to him, pinched his earlobes, and kissed him, nibbling his lips again, gazing at him with silent complicity, then without saying anything, she rose, grabbed her blanket off the floor, plucked the lantern off the dresser, bent down to kiss his cock, and left.

Before he'd finished listening to her bare feet padding down the creaking stairs, Longarm was visited with a rush of racking guilt. He knew it was mere vanity, for his guilt had done nothing to prevent him from fucking Grassley's wife in the first place, but it hammered him nevertheless. Their coupling had sufficiently worn him out, however. He managed to drift back to the blissful dullness of exhausted sleep only fifteen minutes later.

When he woke again, it was still dark, but his body's clock told him it was dawn. Washing with the near-frozen water in the basin topping a tin-covered washstand, he noted the unusual heavy silence. The wind had stopped battering the cabin. When he'd finished washing his face and his cock and balls, he looked out the room's single small square window.

Most of the sky was deep purple. The far eastern horizon was a shade lighter.

Dawn was on its way.

Back to work . . .

Guilt had resumed pestering Longarm the minute he'd awakened, as though someone were poking knitting needles against the back of his neck. The guilt was aggravated by the fact that he was enjoying the remembered images of his and Bettina's fucking. Noting the pull of her in his pants, he shamefully descended downstairs. The kitchen was in a predawn fog despite long orange flames dancing in the parlor's hearth and more orange flames showing around the doors of the range's firebox.

Atop the range, a large black coffeepot chugged softly, slowly, pale steam slithering from its spout.

A figure sat at the oilcloth-covered table. Longarm was trying to form the words with which to greet the woman he'd sinned with only a few hours before, but then he was somewhat relieved to see that it was not Bettina sitting there, after all.

In a voice that resembled the huskiness of the mulatto woman's, however, Miss Evangeline said over the rim of her steaming coffee cup, "Have a good time last night? Or was it early this morning? Maybe both, eh? Seemed to go on a long time."

Longarm cursed. "Was it that loud?"

"Loud enough for me to hear. You two were really going at it. Is that what you do—cuckold men in their own homes?"

Longarm walked over to the door and pulled his heavy coat off its peg. "Don't judge lest ye be judged, teacher." He'd wrapped some steel around "teacher." It was not to his credit that he'd done so, for the woman's circumstances were likely little of her own making, but he was in a sour mood. Besides, he might die today. In a few hours, in fact. Dying and doing what he'd done last night—despite his having enjoyed it so much and was even enjoying it now as he remembered it—were enough to put a chip on any man's shoulder.

"Touché," the teacher said. "Coffee?"

Longarm was buttoning his coat. "No thanks."

She looked up at him—a pretty, brown-haired woman with blue eyes and a pale, heart-shaped face. He could barely make out her cuts and bruises in the dim light. But he could tell that her gaze was wry, a by-product of her calling. "Are you going to do what I think you're going to do? Face those killers yourself?"

"You know how else to root them out of the Blue Dog?"

"Their friends might have shown up by now."

"In this weather?" Longarm said, reaching for his scarf. "I don't think so. If any horseback riders were out in that storm last night, they and their horses are most likely froze up harder than a hangman's heart."

The teacher shook her head slowly, gravely. "If you're expecting any help once you get to town, forget it. All the men in town are cut from the same cloth as our constable."

"That's usually how it is."

Miss Evangeline rose from her chair. She wore a baggy flannel nightgown that caressed the pleasant lumps of her body. She came around the table, reached up, and wrapped her arms around the big lawman's neck. She drew his head down to hers, and she kissed him softly.

"For luck," she said. "And for saving my life." She canted her head to indicate the back of the silent cabin. "Maybe even for saving hers."

Miss Evangeline returned to her seat at the table.

"If yours is somehow miraculously spared, you can save mine again." She smiled—a brief flash of her white teeth over the mug in her hands. And then she took another sip of her coffee.

"I'll take you up on that," Longarm said, shouldering his rifle and opening the door.

"Good-bye."

Chapter 16

"Ugly old woman!" Emory Drake said. "You're not only ugly *and* old, but you can't dance for shit!"

With that, Drake released Miss Jenny, who'd been forced to dance with the man since he and Jenkins had no one else to dance with, and buried his right fist in Jenny's round, soft belly.

"*Ohh!*" the owner of the Blue Dog grunted as the savage blow forced the air from her lungs and she jack-knifed, dropping to her knees on the saloon's rough wooden floor.

Curly Jenkins, his ear bandaged from the bullet he'd taken on the saloon's back stairs, had been playing the piano. If you could call it playing. Mostly, he'd been drunkenly hammering the keys and singing as badly as he'd played while swilling tangleleg to keep his ear from hurting as well as to fight the boredom of the long winter storm while he and Drake waited for the rest of their gang to show up.

As Jenny, trying in vain to suck air into her lungs, rolled onto her right side, Drake gave a cackling, evil laugh, and buried his right boot in her belly.

"*Ohhh!*" Jenny sobbed again as the half a breath she was managing to draw was hammered out of her.

She writhed and groaned and tried desperately to drag air into her lungs. She rolled onto her back and then onto her other shoulder, and then, finally, she managed to draw a raking half breath into her body. Vaguely, beneath her own convulsions, she could hear Drake and Jenkins laughing and stomping around drunkenly. Jenny rolled onto her back, and horror rolled through her at what she saw hanging suspended in the air above her:

Poor little Miss Watson—or whoever she was—the pretty girl who'd entered the saloon with the now-dead preacher—or whatever he was—was hanging from a beam above and to the right of the piano. Drake and Jenkins had hanged her after she'd passed out from exhaustion and could no longer play the piano, which they'd demanded she do out of pure devilishness. They hadn't even been dancing to the music. They'd just said it relaxed them and helped them concentrate on their cards, and they'd demanded she keep playing or they'd shoot her.

But then the girl had passed out and fell to the floor and they'd kicked her and punched her and then finally, when they couldn't rouse her, they fetched a rope and hanged her while Jenny did nothing but beg and plead for her life, on her knees in front of the bar.

That had happened last night. Both men were owly from the encounter with the man out back—the stranger who'd carted Miss Evangeline away in the storm. And then they'd stripped and hanged the pretty little girl. Now the girl's dirty bare feet hung suspended in the air about seven feet above Jenny's head. Her head was tipped forward and to one side, her eyes appearing to stare forlornly out from between the scraggly, disheveled wings of her blond hair.

"Oh," Jenny said, shuttling her gaze to the two killers. "Oh, you devils!"

Fury overwhelmed her once more. Fury and guilt over her inability to prevent the girl's death, or the preacher's death, or the lawmen's deaths.

Again, she said, "Oh, you devils!" but neither man heard it because, she suddenly realized, her lungs were so constricted that the words had probably sounded like strangling. And the men were laughing and stumbling around, kicking chairs—generally being so loud that they couldn't have heard anything except their own guffaws.

But then Drake stumbled over toward the front of the room and, looking out through the frosted glass panes, grew suddenly quiet.

Jenkins had just drawn his long-barreled pistol and was staggering toward Jenny, spinning the gun's cylinder, which made an angry, menacing whine. "I'm tired of lookin' at this old bitch," he raked out, red-faced with sudden rage. "I think I'm gonna—"

"Shut up and get over here!" Drake admonished him.

Jenkins had just leveled his pistol at Jenny's head. Jenny had closed her eyes to accept the bullet and to welcome death, but when she opened them, she saw

Jenkins spinning away from her and stumbling toward his partner, who was now standing at one of the big windows to the right of the front door.

"What the hell is it?" Jenkins asked, his voice echoing around the room that was suddenly quiet except for Jenny's strangled rasps. "That bastard that shot my ear all to hell back?"

"Not that I can tell." Drake turned his head this way and that, looking up and down the street. "What *I* can tell, though, is it's dawn. And the storm's died. Clear as a bell."

"What—you think we should go lookin' for him?"

"Yeah," Drake grunted. "I think we should go lookin' for him. He was here once. He'll likely be back. I say we go out and meet him."

"Ah, hell!" Jenkins wheeled and stumbled over to the bar. He leaned his elbows on the bar top and took his head in his hands, raking his hands brusquely through his curly red hair. "We musta drunk a coupla barrels of that old woman's demon wash. Shit, my head feels six sizes too big for my hat!"

Drake turned toward Jenkins. He, too, was unsteady on his feet. "We gotta sober up, Curly. We gotta sober up now. We gotta assume that son of a bitch will be back here to fix us for the teacher. He might have beat on a few doors and found maybe one, two other men in this jerkass town that got some spine. We gotta sober up, Curly!"

"Yeah, well, tell me how we gonna do that."

Jenny sat up against the piano, one hand on her chest, still trying to catch her breath and wincing against the pain in her belly. She glared at the two men standing at the bar. They seemed oblivious to her presence.

"Here's how we're gonna do it," Drake said, stepping back, spreading his feet, and bunching his fists.

Jenkins scowled at him, incredulous. "Huh?"

He'd barely gotten it out before Drake belted him hard across his left cheek. The blow evoked a started, anguished squeal from Jenkins, who spun around, slamming his chin on the bar top.

"Ouch! Goddamnit, Emory—what in the hell you do that for?" Jenkins was holding a hand across the nub of his left cheek.

"All right," Drake said, bracing himself. "My turn. Give me one, Curly. Come on. Smack me good!"

"You're crazy, Emory!" Jenkins worked his jaw. "I think all the whiskey done turned your brain to mush." He rolled his eyes around, frowning, smiling. "But I'll be damned if my head don't seem clearer!"

"I told you," Drake said, rolling his heavy shoulders, preparing himself for the blow. "Tattoo me good . . . right here!" He tapped his own left cheek.

"All right—you asked for it, you crazy son of a bitch!"

Smack!

Jenkins punched Drake so hard that the stockier, heavier man gave a shrill yelp and, clutching his left jaw, flew several feet back away from the bar and hit the floor on his butt.

He lay flat on his back, caressing his jaw, chest and belly rising and falling sharply.

"You son of a bitch, Curly," he grated out. "I think you came about that far from breaking my jaw clean off my face!" He sat up, working his lower jaw. Blood dribbled from a three-inch gash and bruise on his left cheek.

"But I'll be damned if that didn't clean out the cobwebs!"

Jenkins laughed. Drake climbed heavily to his feet. They gathered their heavy coats and fur hats and their rifles, and, cocking their rifles, they headed out into the lightening dawn.

They must have forgotten about Jenny, who sat as before, pressing her back up taut against the piano, beneath the hanging girl. She glanced up at the girl's small, dirty bare feet, and then she looked out the windows at the front of the saloon. She could hear the outlaws' voices, but she could no longer see them. They must have separated and were moving off along the street.

As quickly as she could, her belly sore and her lungs feeling as though she'd been belted across the chest with an axe handle, Jenny heaved herself to her feet, using the piano bench for leverage. She limped to the back of the saloon and opened the back door.

A drift of snow tumbled in over the doorjamb, covering her boots. She cursed and, shivering against the bone-splintering cold, tramped out into the deep snow under the stairs angling down from the second story.

She kicked around for a time, throwing her arms out for balance and grunting with the effort of the search. Finally, she kicked something yielding beneath the snow, got down on her hands and knees, and thrust her bare hands into the snow. She shivered as she felt around, and her hands quickly turned numb. The discomfort was worth it when, after nearly a minute of probing, she lifted a snowy pistol of one of the dead men out of a four-foot drift.

Clutching the revolver to her heavy bosom, Jenny heaved herself to her feet with a curse and retreated back into the saloon, pulling the door closed with effort against the snow that covered the jamb. Breathless, she turned and looked toward the front of the place. The long room was in shadow. The hanging girl's naked body was also in shadow, though she was turning lighter now as the sun continued to rise, spreading its strengthening light across the clear, green sky vaulting over the chilly-looking false facades on the street's other side.

Still clutching the cold pistol to her bosom, Jenny made her way to the bar. She set down the pistol. Grabbing a shot glass, she filled it hastily, tossed back the shot. She sighed and smacked her lips. She gritted her teeth as she turned her gaze back to the windows facing the street.

"When you two sons of bitches come back here," she said, "I'm gonna blow you straight back to the hell you came from!"

The Percheron leaped and jumped through the high, wavelike drifts capping the ridge on the far side of the creek bottom from the Grassley cabin. Longarm leaned forward to prevent being thrown from the beast's broad back and into the snow that would likely swallow him like quicksand.

A quicksand of tiny frozen diamonds.

In places, the snow appeared five, maybe six feet deep. Fortunately, however, yesterday's wind had also swept the ground between the highest drifts nearly clean in places. There was no clear place on the ridge, but after the Percheron had bulled its way through the deep drifts capping the ridge crest, it picked its way through the valleys that the wind had made between the waves of the white ocean that spread out in all directions around Longarm.

The vast snowfield was dark blue now at dawn, but that blue was gradually lightening, and each individual flake of the freshly fallen snow was beginning to sparkle. The cold was a palpable menace, pushing through Longarm's heavy winter attire, chewing on his nose like a rabid dog, nipping at his fingers and toes. His and the horse's breaths jetted into the gradually brightening air around them.

As Longarm approached the edge of the snow-socked town—which appeared more snow now than wood and brick, with here and there smoke rising from brick chimneys or tin chimney pipes—the sun cleared the horizon. The buttery glow shone suddenly on the highest points of the buildings ahead of him—on the tallest barns and shops, anyway, while leaving the smaller hovels purple where they hunched in the nearly roof-deep snow.

As hovels started pushing up around Longarm and the trudging horse, the sun glistened in the corner of the lawman's right eye. The large, buttery orb was on the rise, though it didn't seem to be warming the air much. The temperature was probably around zero. Longarm slipped into the deep shade of a three-story wood-frame shop on his right. As he did, he removed the mitten from over his right glove. He pocketed the mitten, reached forward, slid his Winchester from its leather scabbard, cocked the rifle one-handed, and rested it across his saddlebow. No sooner had he made the move than he saw the flicker of a shadow in a window of the three-story shop.

He jerked his head in that direction, raising the Winchester's barrel. A long, pale, craggy face—the face of an old man—stared out at him. Longarm frowned, scrutinizing the face. Then he saw that the old man's right hand was bobbing up and down, extended thump pointing up.

Just as Longarm realized that the oldster was indicating the roof of the shop, the sun basted that same roof in liquid gold. Javelins of the bright light stabbed Longarm's eyes a half second after he'd glimpsed a man-shaped silhouette against it—complete with bristling rifle!

Longarm tried to raise his own Winchester but the bright sunlight was like a physical blow, dazzling him. Orange fireworks blossomed against his retinas.

The rifle on the roof cracked sharply, loudly. At the same time, what felt like a powerful, brass-knuckled fist, but which the lawman knew was a bullet, punched his left arm, throwing that arm out wide and, a quarter second later, sending the rest of the lawman flying off the Percheron's back with an anguished, startled groan.

Chapter 17

Longarm arced away from the horse and into snow, which plumed around him like fresh down, cushioning his fall but enveloping him in its giant icy palm. The Percheron gave a shrill whinny, pitched sharply, and then ran, buck-kicking, straight ahead toward where the side street intersected the main drag.

As Longarm tried to scramble to his feet, slipping and sliding in the deep, suffocating snow but managing to hold on to his Winchester, the other rifle belched again.

The bullet whispered wickedly through the snow before the dull thud of its meeting with the frozen ground made its way to Longarm's ringing ears. The lawman grunted, breathing hard, as he scrambled to his feet and plowed madly through the snow, making for a gap between two small wood-framed shops opposite the three-story shop from which the shots had been fired.

The rifle spoke again. The bullet clipped Longarm's left heel, tripping him.

The lawman hit the snow again, twisting around onto his back and raising his rifle toward the orange ball of the sun engulfing the three-story shop's roof. Squinting against the glare, he could make out the figure silhouetted against it, and he triggered two quick, angry shots at it.

Then he turned and scrambled back to his feet and ran into the gap between the buildings, diving the last few feet from the gap's mouth as the opposing rifle cracked two more times, sending its wicked echoes screeching over the snow-locked town. One slug hammered the corner of the building on Longarm's right, blowing wood slivers into the snow near Longarm's airborne heels.

The lawman hit the ground and rolled up against the base of the building on his right, gripping his rifle tightly in his hands and snaking his right gloved finger through the trigger guard. He cocked a fresh cartridge into the chamber and looked back toward the three-story building. He couldn't see the roof from this vantage, which meant the shooter couldn't see him, either.

He winced at the painful throb in his left arm. Blood oozed from a hole in his buckskin, painting the snow that enfolded him like a goose down quilt. The blood was cold and wet against his arm, inside his coat. Knowing he had to stem the tide of spilling blood, he quickly leaned his rifle against the wall of the building behind him. He opened his coat, then pulled a neckerchief out of a pocket and reached into the coat to tie the cloth around the wound.

He threw his head back and rasped out several sharp curses as, one-handed, he knotted the neckerchief tightly around the throbbing hole. While the wound hurt like hell, the lawman had been hit enough times in the past to deem the bone unbroken. The bullet had probably taken a nick out of it, but it had likely mostly only plowed through flesh before exiting.

Longarm buttoned the coat, lifted its collar up around his jaws and the scarf doing its best to keep his neck from getting frostbit, and then grabbed his rifle. As he did, he edged back to the street and looked toward the sunlit top of the building once more.

Something moved along the building's peak. The sunlight was no longer as intense as before. He could make out a hat, a fringe of red beard, and the guidon-like end of a green scarf blowing in the cold breeze.

Then he saw the rifle being leveled over the peak.

Being aimed in his direction . . .

Longarm sucked a sharp, angry breath, raised his own rifle to his shoulder, aimed hastily, and fired once, twice, three times. The first and second bullets tore up wood just beneath the building's peak and the figure hunkered atop it. The third bullet must have struck pay dirt, because the rifle was suddenly jerked up as it was fired skyward, and then pulled down with the rest of the bastard wielding it as the shooter dropped down behind the building's peak.

Longarm sucked another anxious breath and began scrambling to his feet. He'd likely wounded the shooter, but how bad? Longarm decided he'd circle the little building, taking an unpredictable route, and find out.

Just as he'd turned to run toward the building's rear, he stopped. A stocky man in a striped blanket coat had just slipped around the rear corner. He wore a fur cap

with earflaps that appeared to be a size too small for his
large head and broad, mustached face. As he dipped his
chin toward the stock of the rifle he was aiming at Longarm, Longarm threw himself to the side.

He hit the snow on his right arm and rolled as the
stocky gent's rifle belched twice, both slugs tearing up
snow at Longarm's feet. Longarm rolled up onto his left
knee, quickly leveled his own repeater, and fired three
shots, the cartridge casings arcing over his right shoulder to bounce off the wooden wall behind him. The
bullets tore chunks of wood from the rear corner of the
other building and sent the second shooter staggering
back around the corner and out of sight.

Longarm thought he'd heard the man give a pained
yelp.

The lawman gritted his teeth against the throb in his
left arm. He stole forward through the snow, quickly
pinching fresh cartridges from his shell belt beneath his
coat and thumbing them into the Winchester's loading
gate. The heat of the gun felt good in his cold right hand.

He glanced back toward the street, making sure the
first shooter wasn't drawing another bead on him.

As he punched the last cartridge into the Winchester,
he levered a round into the chamber and leveled the gun
as he bounded around the building's rear corner. He
tightened his trigger finger but then eased the tension.

The shooter was gone. Nothing but rumpled snow
and a few pink splotches that could only be the redness
of diluted blood. The tracks trailed around a small stable
with a padlocked door and connecting corral, which
was empty.

Longarm would deal with the second son of a bitch

after he'd made sure he'd beefed the first son of a bitch . . .

To that end, he walked around the small building's opposite corner and made his way through the deep snow swelling up along its northeast wall. As he approached the front, he swept his eyes across the front of the three-story shop rising on the other side of the street. He could see the building clearly now, for the sun wasn't nearly as intense as before. Gray smoke lifted from a brick chimney. That appeared to be the only movement.

Longarm started forward, stopped.

He'd been wrong. The smoke wasn't the only movement. A figure just now came around from behind the building and was aiming a rifle along the side of the three-story structure toward Longarm, who dropped quickly down behind a frozen rain barrel.

The shooter's rifle cracked. The slug plowed into the opposite side of the frozen barrel from Longarm with a wicked, crackling *pop*, causing the barrel to shiver and lose some of the snow capping it. Longarm waited for another shot. When it didn't come, he snaked his rifle around the barrel's left side, and, only half aiming, cut loose with three staccato blasts.

He pulled his rifle back behind the barrel, kept his head down for about fifteen seconds, and then risked a look over the top.

Nothing.

He fired another two rounds, hoping to flush his quarry. When that didn't work, he glanced behind him, making sure the second son of a bitch wasn't about to drill him between the shoulder blades, then bounded out from behind the barrel and ran heavily, clumsily through the snow. The fresh, wind-whipped powder was only about knee-deep in the street, so he increased his pace despite the sharp throbbing in his wounded arm.

He ran down the side of the three-story building, saw the place in the snow where the first shooter had stood when he'd fired at Longarm a second time. He followed the man's long, furrowed tracks to the rear of the place, where the man lay in a small area that the wind had swept nearly clean of snow about three feet from the base of a sprawling cottonwood, its branches crusted with ice.

The man lay on his back, hands lifted to his neck. He was kicking his feet and generally jerking all over as blood welled from the hole that Longarm had drilled through the dead center of the man's throat. He was a tall hombre, brown-eyed, with frizzy red hair. He'd lost his hat, though a ratty green scarf was tied over his head from crown to jaw. His rifle lay beside him against the frozen yellow grass crusted with old snow.

The killer stared up at Longarm, brown eyes bright with horror. He was moving his lips, trying to speak, but only gurgling and frothy blood bubbled out, oozing over his chin and down the front of his wool coat.

Longarm looked all around, making sure that he and the dying man were alone. Then he turned back to the dying man and said, "What kind of man would treat a woman the way you do?" he asked, shaking his head slowly with bald disdain. "Yellow-livered, bottom-feeding scum—that's who."

The man continued to move his lips. He lifted a wool-gloved hand toward Longarm, pleading for help.

"You won't get any help from me," Longarm said, sliding shells through his Winchester's loading gate and looking cautiously around. "If you're still alive when I get back, after I've finished your friends, I'll drill a bullet through your head. If you haven't bled dry or frozen to death, either of which you'll likely do before then. No point in trying to keep a dead man alive. That's as far as I'll go for a yellow dog like you."

Longarm turned and headed back out to the street.

The dying man continued to gurgle and sputter and bleed out behind him.

Standing behind the bar of the Blue Dog Saloon, Jenny stiffened.

She'd heard the crunching thuds of running feet rising from the snowy main street, and now she saw the bulky figure of Emory Drake come running into view from the south. He was running loosely, elbows and knees akimbo. At first, Jenny thought he was running awkwardly on account of the snow.

But then her heart quickened. Her lower jaw loosened when she saw that the rapist and cold-blooded killer was occasionally grabbing at his upper right side, somewhere under his right arm, and that his coat there glistened with fresh blood. He held his rifle loosely in his right hand. He leaped up onto the porch, tripping and dropping out of Jenny's sight for a second, before bulling both winter doors wide open.

The cold blew in with him. Cold and the snow falling from his clothes.

Jenny had considered barring the door on the man.

But then she'd reconsidered. She reached under the bar to wrap her right hand around the grips of the pistol she'd exhumed from the snow.

How could she kill him if she didn't let him back inside?

Drake stopped just inside the gaping doors and dropped to one knee, breathing hard.

No, Jenny thought. *Don't you die there. Not there and not now. I want to be the one to kill you, goddamnit!*

She'd heard the muffled reports of the shooting, of course. The air was so cold and still in the wake of the storm that everyone had likely heard the shots.

Now, trying not to sound overly mocking, she said, "You run into a puma out there, did you? One as good with a gun as you fellas?"

Drake merely glanced at her. To him, she was no more than a bothersome fly. He obviously had more important matters on his mind.

He heaved himself to his feet, turned, and stepped back between the open doors, looking down the street in the direction from which he'd run. As he did, he cupped his left hand to his right side, up high beneath his arm. Same side that the Reverend had stabbed him. Jenny saw the skin curl back along his jaw. He was wincing from the pain.

That the man was in pain eased Jenny's heart. She squeezed the handle of the revolver on the top shelf beneath the bar. She caressed the uncocked hammer with her thumb. She had to get in close before she'd take a chance at squeezing off a shot. You had to be good to hit what you were shooting at with a pistol, and Jenny had rarely fired anything but her old stolen shotgun. And her eyes weren't as good as they once had been.

She had to get close or she'd miss and he'd kill her.

"Puma?" Drake said, facing the street, his voice pinched slightly with pain. "Nah. Not a puma. Just a man with a rifle. He's good with that rifle, by God." He glanced over his shoulder at Jenny, showed her a cock-eyed grin. "But if Curly don't get him, the bastard—whoever he is—will follow me here, and I'll have the honor."

He winked but Jenny could tell he was scared. That warmed her even more. Drake turned back to the street. As he studied the snowy trace now glittering like a giant quilt woven with diamonds, he began to reload his Winchester carbine from his shell belt, working methodically, keeping an eye on the street.

Jenny started to pull the gun out from under the bar but stopped when Drake said, "Bring me a bottle, woman."

Jenny tensed, thoughts racing.

Drake turned to glare at her over his shoulder. "Whiskey! *Now!*"

"All right," Jenny said, putting every ounce of her energy into trying to remain calm. "Hold your horses. I don't move as fast as I used to."

Drake scoffed as he turned his head back toward the street, looking cautiously around. Meanwhile, Jenny pulled the pistol off the shelf.

Chapter 18

Gun in her right hand, a fresh whiskey bottle in her left hand, Jenny started to walk out from behind the bar. She was glad when something caught Drake's attention along the main street to the south.

He stepped out from between the doors and turned to stare furtively, tensely in that direction, holding his rifle across his chest. His breath feathered away in the chill breeze, limned in golden morning sunshine.

Jenny walked up to the door.

Her heart was pounding. Her feet felt like mud in her boots.

"Here's your whiskey, you son of a bitch!"

She tossed the bottle through the open doors, across the stoop, and into the snow just beyond the porch steps. Drake glanced back at her. He looked at the bottle and then turned sharply back to Jenny, scowling, the muscles in his jaws bulging.

"What'd you call . . . ?" Drake let his voice trail off

when he saw the pistol in the woman's hands. He jerked with a start and then turned to square his shoulders at her.

Jenny raised the pistol in both her hands, ratcheting back the hammer.

"Whoa, now, woman," Drake said, his voice pitched with mockery. "You be careful there. You sure you know what you're doin' with that thing?"

"I don't know," Jenny said, her old heart racing. She tried to keep her hands from shaking as she raised the pistol and aimed at the killer's forehead, just beneath his fur-lined cap. "I reckon we'll see."

"Whoa, now!" Drake yelled as Jenny squeezed the trigger.

She closed her eyes and turned away slightly as the revolver roared in her hands. The gun's kick rocked her back on her heels and sent her stumbling backward into the saloon. She opened her eyes and heard herself gasp when she saw Drake still standing.

The killer was facing her but with his head half turned.

A long, dark line angled across the nub of his left cheek all the way to his ear. As Jenny stared at it, aghast, blood began to ooze out along the line to bead along the line, then slowly dribble down the man's weather-darkened cheek.

Drake blinked once, slowly, and then he glared at Jenny. "You fuckin' bitch," he said slowly, with quiet menace, walking toward her, holding his rifle down low in his right hand.

Jenny raised the pistol once more, ratcheting the hammer back.

"Don't you do it!" Drake roared, thrusting a warning finger at her.

Jenny tried to keep her eyes open this time as she aimed again at Drake's forehead and squeezed the trigger.

To her horror, the revolver did not roar but made a quiet belching sound on the heels of the tinny click of the hammer dropping down onto the firing pin. Jenny's lower jaw dropped in shock and horror as she stared at the benign weapon in her shaking hands.

Drake laughed. "You find that out in the snow?" He laughed again. "Why, the cartridge was fouled!"

Jenny cursed as she madly tried to ratchet the hammer back once more. Drake closed his hand over the top of the pistol, jerked it out of her hand, and flung it across the room. Then he raised his rifle, planting the barrel firmly against her forehead.

Jenny closed her eyes and tried to calmly accept the bullet. *It's all right,* she silently told herself. *I'm off to be reunited with Abigail . . .*

She closed her eyes and drew a deep, calming breath.

"Put the gun down," a deep, resonate, unfamiliar voice said. "Put it down now or I'll blow the back of your head apart, Drake."

Drake pulled the rifle away from Jenny's head. He whipped around toward the tall man standing in the open doorway, boots spread, his own Winchester aimed straight out from his shoulder at Drake. He was a tall, mustached man wearing a flat-brimmed black hat, red scarf, and a bulky buckskin mackinaw. The left arm of the mackinaw was bloodstained.

His tough brown eyes were riveted on Drake, who

gave a scream as he raised his own Winchester only to go dancing backward and drop his rifle as the tall stranger's own rifle spat smoke and fire.

There were three loud, building-rocking blasts.

Jenny stumbled backward, fell to the floor, and buried her face in her arms, hearing beneath the blasts of the rifle the decisive *whumps!* of the stranger's bullets slamming through the howling Drake.

There was one last loud thud, which Jenny assumed was the killer hitting the floor.

Boots thudded toward Jenny. She looked up at the tall man standing over her. He was silhouetted against the brightly lit doorway behind him. He dropped to one knee beside her, extended his gloved right hand.

"You all right, ma'am?"

Jenny nodded. But then her gut soured when she saw a group of fur-coated men on horseback—a dozen men, at least—pull their horses up to the hitchrack fronting the saloon.

Every man in the group was holding a rifle. And every man was casting his cold-eyed gaze at the saloon where their leader, Emory Drake, lay dead as rotten beef.

Jenny nodded at the stranger, swallowed. "For now," she said. "But neither of us is gonna be all right for long, I'm afraid, mister."

Longarm wheeled, racking a fresh round into his Winchester's breech.

He cast his gaze through the open doors and through the windows on either side of the doorway. His guts writhed around in his belly as he walked through the doors to stand on the stoop, spreading his boots and holding his rifle in both hands across high thighs.

Twelve men sat their horses, facing him. Their breaths plumed around their bearded heads. Their flat, glassy eyes regarded him with cool disdain. To a man, they were wielding either Winchester or Henry rifles.

One man in the middle of the pack—a green-eyed hombre with a dragoon-style frost-rimed mustache—said, "Who the fuck are you?"

Longarm told him. They all looked around at each other, frowning.

"Where's Drake?" asked the same man who'd spoken before.

"Dead. So's Jenkins. I'm assuming McKirk's dead, too, since I haven't seen him by now."

"He is," the older woman called from the shadows of the saloon behind Longarm.

"Yep, I was right," Longarm said, his smile belying his apprehension.

He had no doubt that he was about to die. But he sure as hell wasn't going alone.

He took one more step forward, until he was standing at the top of the porch steps, within six feet of the nearest mounted outlaw. "You fellas drop those rifles."

"What's that?" asked one of the other gang members, grinning. His lips and shaggy ginger beard were coated with frost and frozen tobacco juice.

"You heard me. Drop them rifles. Then toss down your other weapons, too. You're all under arrest, see? I'm takin' you in."

The gang members looked around at each other once more, grinning, chuckling. Then the man with the droopy mustache who Longarm assumed was the leader of this branch of the gang said, "Mister, either you ain't alone here, or you're a fuckin' moron."

"Well, I reckon I'm alone here," Longarm said. "Whether the other's true, I guess I'm not in a position to judge."

"He's neither," said a voice somewhere off to Longarm's far left.

Just then, bundled in a heavy coat and fur hat, Emmitt Grassley stepped out from behind the Blue Dog's front corner. He loudly cocked the rifle in his hands.

"No, he ain't alone!" This was a woman's voice. Longarm watched Bettina Grassley step out from behind the corner of the hotel on the other side of the street and a little left of the Blue Dog. She, too, held a rifle in her hands. She cocked her weapon now as well, and raised it to her shoulder.

Boots thudded behind Longarm.

"Nope, he ain't alone," said the woman from inside the saloon. She came up to stand at Longarm's right. She glanced at him, winked, and then cocked Emory Drake's rifle and raised it to her shoulder, aiming at one of the gang members gathered in front of the porch.

There was a wooden scraping sound. Longarm looked across the street to see one of the hotel's third-story windows open. Miss Evangeline ducked her head through the opening, raising a rifle to her cheek.

The window beside her opened as well. Beyond it, Longarm saw what he thought was the same long gray face he'd glimpsed in the other three-story building earlier—the man who'd warned him about Jenkins perched on the roof above him.

The old man extended a Sharps carbine through the open window, angling it down toward the gang, wisps of his gray hair blowing out around the top of his nearly bald head.

The gang turned their horses this way and that, getting a look at all the armed people around and above them. Their horses whinnied and hopped nervously around in the deep snow, betraying the sudden edginess of the men on their backs.

"Lookee here," Longarm said. "I got me a whole passel of deputies, and I didn't even know it." He glanced at Grassley and Bettina and then shuttled his gaze from Miss Evangeline to the old man and to the woman from the saloon. He gave the woman a wink.

And then he turned to the gang. "You fellas ready to drop them rifles now?"

The leader raked his gaze around at the rifles aimed at him. He silently conferred with the other nervous men around him.

"Nope," he said, shaking his head and bunching his lips. "No, we sure ain't!"

He jerked his rifle down, but before he could squeeze off a shot, Longarm's Winchester sent him hurling off the back of his horse and into the heavy snow. And then there followed what sounded like a small but fierce battle.

And a brief one, too.

In less than two minutes, nearly all of the gang's horses were milling restlessly and riderless in the snowy street—those that hadn't galloped off during the shooting, that is. One of the gang members had been shot out of his saddle like the others, but, getting his boot caught in a stirrup, was dragged off to the south behind his frightened, buck-kicking mount.

As the smoke wafted in the cold air over the street, Longarm heaved himself up against the awning support post behind which he'd taken cover while emptying both his Winchester and Colt revolver into the gang, then gave the woman from the saloon a hand up as well.

"You all right, ma'am?" he asked her.

"Fit as a fiddle," she said, looking around with a dazed but relieved look at all the dead men sprawled in the bloody snow. "And . . . uh . . . the name's Jenny. I own this here watering hole."

"Had a feelin' you did," Longarm said. "I'm Longarm."

The two shook hands warmly.

When Longarm saw that all of his "deputies" looked as unscathed as Miss Jenny, he gave in to the burning throb in his left arm and staggered inside the saloon and up to the bar. Before, he'd glimpsed the naked girl hanging near the piano, but now he inspected her more closely.

Recognizing the face as well as the body, he shook his head fatefully and turned back to the bar.

"I believe I'll have a drink," he told Miss Jenny.

"Well, I believe you deserve one, Longarm."

"As do you, Miss Jenny. Help yourself. I'm buyin'."

"Don't mind if I do. But, please—on me."

They touched shot glasses and sipped their drinks. As they did, Emmitt Grassley came in, looking sheepish. He sidled up to the bar, waved off the drink that Jenny offered, and extended his hand to Longarm.

"Thanks, Custis."

Frowning dubiously but shaking the man's hand automatically, the federal lawman said, "What on earth for, Emmitt?"

"For helping me pull my man pants on."

Just then, Bettina came in. She glanced from her husband to Longarm and back again. She encircled one of Grassley's arms with her own and smiled at him. "Come on. Let's get you home."

She glanced once more at Longarm. Her brown eyes grew even brighter as they took in her husband once more. "Let's get us both home," she said.

Grassley and Bettina left the saloon arm in arm.

As they did, Miss Evangeline walked in, leaning her rifle against the wall and lowering the hood of her heavy wool cape. The teacher smiled at Miss Jenny and then she walked over to stand beside Longarm.

She looked at the bloody sleeve of his coat and said, "Looks like your life could use some saving, mister."

"You know—I reckon it could at that, teacher."

Longarm threw back the last of his drink, pinched his hat brim to Miss Jenny, and then he and Miss Evangeline headed for the stairs.

Watch for

LONGARM AND THE DEATH CAVE

the 428th novel in the exciting LONGARM
series from Jove

Coming in July!

GIANT-SIZED ADVENTURE FROM
AVENGING ANGEL LONGARM.

BY TABOR EVANS

2006 Giant Edition:

LONGARM AND THE
OUTLAW EMPRESS

2007 Giant Edition:

LONGARM AND
THE GOLDEN EAGLE
SHOOT-OUT

2008 Giant Edition:

LONGARM AND THE
VALLEY OF SKULLS

2009 Giant Edition:

LONGARM AND THE
LONE STAR TRACKDOWN

2010 Giant Edition:

LONGARM AND THE
RAILROAD WAR

2013 Giant Edition:

LONGARM AND
THE AMBUSH AT HOLY
DEFIANCE

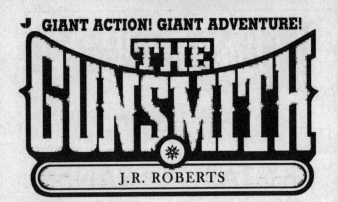

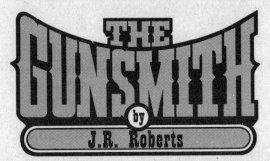